# HIGH, WIDE AND HANDSOME

Center Point
Large Print

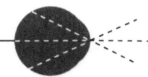

**This Large Print Book carries the Seal of Approval of N.A.V.H.**

# HIGH, WIDE AND HANDSOME

## Curt Brandon

CENTER POINT LARGE PRINT
THORNDIKE, MAINE

To
H. B. DUNAGAN, JR.
*At least he's wide.*
*And he'll do to ride the river with.*

This Center Point Large Print edition
is published in the year 2024 by arrangement with
Golden West Inc.

Copyright © 1950 by Curt Brandon.
Copyright © renewed 1978 by Curt Brandon.

All rights reserved.

Originally published in the US by
E. P. Dutton & Company, Inc.

The text of this Large Print edition is unabridged.
In other aspects, this book may vary
from the original edition.
Printed in the United States of America
on permanent paper sourced using
environmentally responsible foresting methods.
Set in 16-point Times New Roman type.

ISBN 979-8-89164-040-5 (hardcover)
ISBN 979-8-89164-044-3 (paperback)

The Library of Congress has cataloged this record
under Library of Congress Control Number: 2023947768

# CHAPTER ONE

That would have been my last day of school even if my father had not met Tim Mulloy face to face in Yancey's saloon that afternoon.

I had made up my mind to that sometime during that long tortuous day. From where I squirmed on a pine bench I could see the mile-wide hoof-torn trail leading to the Red River and beyond, and from the lips of riders who knew its every turning I had heard yarns of the greatest march of men and beasts the world has ever known. Only the day before Patricia had received a letter from Rich Stewart in the Cimarron—a letter somebody wrote for him since Rich never went a day to school and could only scrawl his name—and Rich had leased a half million acres of land and wanted to buy thirty thousand head of Texas cattle.

All day long I had thought about that letter, and Rich Stewart, and stared at the sun-browned and cattle-scarred trail, the road I would take to the Cimarron, and I had vowed to myself that would be my last day listening to a hook-nosed schoolteacher who had to grab his saddlehorn when his horse broke into a lope.

I had wanted to quit before but Patricia had insisted I had to finish. I don't think my father would have cared if I had thrown my schoolbooks into the teacher's face and gone galloping up the trail without a backward look. Often I overheard him say to Patricia: "A colt must run, sister, a colt must run." But my sister's mouth would go tight and I would know there was nothing ahead of me but the dusty schoolroom overfilled with benches and scarred desks and the reproving glares of that teacher who knew nothing about horses, cows or kids. So I had stayed until I was sixteen.

I might have stayed on except for that letter from Rich—and, of course, Dad's meeting Tim Mulloy in Yancey's. But after hearing of the wide loop Rich was throwing in the Cimarron, I couldn't have stood it another day. A long time before the bell rang that afternoon I had decided to join Rich in the Indian country.

I slammed my books into their box under the desk top the second the bell rang and I ran out of the box frame house without a by-your-leave to Hungry Higgins, the skinny schoolteacher from the East, and I headed for the town of Cotulla at a gallop. I had a twenty-dollar goldpiece in my pocket and a man leaving for the Cimarron before daylight needed some things—shells, for example, and a slab of bacon to carry in his saddlebag.

I saw Dad's horse hitched in front of Yancey's saloon and reined up. Here and now, I thought, was the place and time to talk to him, away from

Patricia's tight lips and severe eyes, while he was in a sympathetic mood. I wasn't afraid of what he would say. I even dared to hope that he would help me handle Patricia.

Usually the saloon at this hour was a bedlam of laughter and talk, but all was still as I stepped inside the door and I saw my father and another man standing at the bar, each with a drink before him but neither touching it. I recognized Tim Mulloy with a sudden twitching of my throat and I understood why the saloon was quiet and the usual drinkers backed away from the bar, waiting still and tense.

Right behind Tim Mulloy stood his cousin, Jeb, and I quickly stepped to Dad's side, though none of them saw me. Even if I didn't have a gun I wasn't going to let my dad be ganged by the Mulloys.

Tim Mulloy didn't notice me. He was a lean man, with sharp-cut features and a thin mouth and dark eyes, jet black eyes. I knew him for the man who had killed my grandfather and I hated him with the sullen unyielding hate only a sixteen-year-old can feel.

"You say you're a peace-loving man, Haines," Mulloy said harshly. I never heard him talk any other way but quick and jerky. "Mebbe so. But you're a Haines and this country is too danged small for the Mulloys and the Haines both."

"Stay on your side of the river," my father

answered evenly, "and I'll stay on my side. That way we won't have trouble."

I was too young then to understand my father, a clear-eyed smiling man who worked hard on our fences and barns, who made money with a small spread even in the dry seasons, and who had never mentioned to me the feud between us and the Mulloys. I had pieced together the story from talk dropped here and there, and from graves marked by small rockslabs on the pasture slope that fell away into the Frio Canyon three hundred feet below. I knew that my grandfather had fallen before Tim's guns in this very saloon and that shifty-eyed Jeb Mulloy never got likkered up without boasting what he would do to any Haines he could lay his hands on.

But my father, to my knowledge, never carried a gun and I never heard him say a word against a Mulloy. He tried to live as if the feud had never happened. Right now, talking pleasantly to Tim, he was as good as asking for peace and an end to the hate that had touched almost every home in the Frio.

But Tim Mulloy would not have it so; that showed in his gleaming eyes and his thin lips.

"It's too late for that, Haines," Tim sneered. "If you're afraid to fight, I'll buy you out at a fair price and you move out of the country. Otherwise I'm asking you to be wearing a gun the next time we meet."

I shivered and looked appraisingly at Jeb. If Dad jumped Tim with his bare hands, or a whiskey bottle, it would be up to me to keep Jeb out of it. I'd dive for his legs, I decided. I'd grab his ankles and . . .

"There is no question of selling," my father answered carefully. "That would be running from you and I can't do that. I'm not a running man either, Mulloy."

He pushed his drink further away; evidently he didn't intend to touch it again. He looked around the saloon, from one expressionless face to the next. I think he realized what they were thinking. Never in this country had a man refused such a challenge. Never in this country had one man talked like Tim Mulloy had to another, and both of them lived.

"I reckon our people had something to fight about when this started," Dad said to Tim, still calm and easy. "It was open country then and I don't hold it against your father that he wanted to spread out. Then a man was entitled to all the grass he could grab and hold. Now, between you and me, there is nothing but an old hate. We're not in each other's way, Tim. You own your land and I own mine and there's a fence between us."

His voice never changed. But I saw his eyebrows drop, which was about the only way he ever showed what he felt.

"But I don't run, Tim," he added gently. "Next time . . . I'll have a gun."

Sometime in this talk he had noticed me. Now he turned away from Tim Mulloy.

"Thought I would wait here and ride home with you, Petey," he said pleasantly, as if he had turned his back only on a casual conversation. "Figured you would notice my horse."

Once more his eyes swept around the saloon. It seemed to me he was a little defiant of them and their code that was the code of their fathers before them. "Adios, men," he said. There were friendly answers. My father was not one of their kind, but they were bound to respect him. He meant what he said. The next time he met Tim Mulloy he would have a gun on him.

We were a half mile out of town before I could talk.

"Gosh, Dad, you didn't let Tim Mulloy scare you a bit, did you?"

He was smoking a cigar as we rode along at an easy trot. He took the cigar out of his mouth and studied it a moment before answering.

Then, "I haven't a chance against Tim Mulloy, Pete," he answered calmly.

I stared at him and the truth of what he said filled me with an empty horror.

"But, Dad . . . !" I protested.

"If by a quick lucky shot," he mused, "I killed Tim first, then I would have Jeb to deal with. Jeb has the reputation of being the best man with a gun in this country."

I had to admit that. Jeb Mulloy had six notches on the handle of his gun.

"Then what are you going to do?" I demanded.

"We'll decide that later," he said. From the tone of his voice I knew he did not want to talk about it anymore. Not then anyhow.

I had chores to do before supper; we kept chickens and a milk cow, one of the few in that country. And, though Patricia planted the garden herself, it was up to me to keep it weeded. This was still another reason why I had been eager to get away to Rich Stewart in the Cimarron. The other boys my age sneered at me for being a "hoe man."

I thought about Rich and the trail to the Red River as I hoed the peas and onions. I couldn't leave before daylight as I had planned. I had to stay and see Dad through his fight with Tim Mulloy. The troubled heart I had felt like an anvil inside my chest. If Dad were killed, I couldn't go at all; I would have to stay there and take care of Patricia. And, I thought miserably, it would be up to me to carry on the feud. It would be up to me to strap a gun around my waist and shoot at Tim Mulloy on sight . . . and be shot at. I can shoot at Tim, I thought, and at his ugly cousin, Jeb. But there was Eddie Mulloy whom everybody called "Skip," a year younger than me. We got along all right at school in spite of the bad blood between our families. Skip was little for his age and had a quick bubbling good humor which wasn't like any other Mulloy I had ever known. He could ride a horse though; he could lean over and snatch up a hat from the ground on a dead run. I wondered if Skip had heard about his dad and mine and was thinking as I was that sooner or later he and I would feel the same way about each other.

I'd buy the shells for my pistol all right, I promised myself. But I wouldn't slip off to the Cimarron before daylight. I'd stay there and practice shooting at prairie dogs and jack rabbits and get ready. Damn the Mulloys, I'd give 'em all they wanted. And if Rich should ever . . .

Dad came to the barn just then and I called to him. "Dad, I got a notion. Why don't you just send for Rich Stewart? Rich would scatter them Mulloys from hell to breakfast."

A faint smile touched his face. He leaned against the corral fence and rolled a cigarette.

"I'm tempted, Pete," he said. "The Mulloys think they're tough, Jeb especially. It would be some fun to see Rich after 'em."

Then, shrugging his shoulders, "But it isn't Rich's battle, Pete. Maybe . . . if he and Pat ever marry . . ."

"We could rush that up," I proposed. "They're

talking about it anyhow. I think she's as good as told him."

His eyes twinkled. "Don't tempt me, Pete," he said again.

But I knew he wasn't tempted; he was enjoying the mental picture of lean Rich Stewart facing Jeb Mulloy in a gun battle, that was all.

I finished the chores and went in to supper. Patricia was putting it on the table and I beamed in anticipation—dried apple pies and berry preserves for dessert. Dad ate rapidly and with little appetite and then he stalked outside. For some reason or other I offered to dry the dishes—a startling offer; it was a wonder Pat didn't faint from the shock. But, instead, she smiled and patted my shoulder.

In my estimation she wasn't such a pretty girl, though nearly all the young men in the Frio Valley seemed to think otherwise. She was tall, with big blue eyes, and I had thought it was silly the way she piled her yellow hair up high and curled long bangs across her forehead. But it was her manner more than her hairdo. . . . Pat seemed to always be looking at the serious side of life, with a kind of a pride about her and a quiet but firm resolve to get her own way. I had overheard one of the Winslow boys say that she was no gal to carry to a dance, but one to marry.

That Winslow had tried, and so had just about every other single man in Frio country, but none of 'em had ever gotten out of the chute. Rich Stewart was the only waddy she had ever sparked with.

Which was funny. I had never seen Rich when he didn't have the gleam of devilment in his eye.

After we finished the dishes Pat sewed on my socks and on Dad's shirts and I fooled with saddle shop catalogues until Dad came back inside. I studied his face as he sat moodily before the fireplace, sometimes holding out his hands as if there were a blaze there. So did Pat, I noticed. But finally he went to bed without a word to either of us.

I followed him. But I didn't get to sleep right away. I kept looking into Tim Mulloy's lean dark face and seeing the gleam of his narrow black eyes.

It was hard to roll out of bed the next morning when Dad called me. But I came wide awake when he said:

"You're not going to school today, Pete. I want you to ride over to Keith Winslow's and ask him to loan us a couple of men today."

We hired only two riders ourselves; on roundups we either put on extra men, when they could be found, or swapped out with our neighbors.

"Yes, sir," I said quickly.

Something was up, I knew. I wolfed my breakfast and galloped over to the Winslow outfit. Keith came himself with two of his hands.

"Your dad must be rounding up early," drawled Keith as we rode along.

I knew what he was thinking. I wanted to throw his quiet suggestion back into his face. Dad wasn't running. I didn't know why the early roundup, but Dad wasn't running.

When we got back there was Ben Otis of the Tall S there with his riders and they were talking about cows and horses.

I looked anxiously at Dad. We were down to stockers mostly, with maybe a hundred two-year-olds. If Dad was selling now, it meant just one thing . . . he was selling out.

"I'll take all you got, Haines," Otis said. He was a big fat man but he wasn't a jovial one.

"Then we'll bring 'em all in," Dad nodded. "We can work this whole range by night."

He turned to Keith, "Much obliged," he said. "You know roundups better than any man in this country, Keith. Suppose you do the ramrodding?"

Keith hesitated. He wanted to say something, and I could guess what. But, instead, he nodded and jerked his horse around and the roundup started.

By mid-afternoon we had pushed everything in a cow's hide into the lower pasture and Otis rode among 'em, jabbing at an animal every now and then with his cane.

"I figger eight hundred and seven," he finally told Dad.

"I'll take your figure, Otis," Dad said quietly. He had been like that all day, not saying a word except when it was absolutely necessary, then talking in a low polite tone. We had ridden back to the house for dinner, eating on the porch where Patricia had set a long table.

Now Dad looked to Keith Winslow. "Otis thinks twenty-two is a fair price," he said. "I'm asking twenty-three fifty."

Business was done that way—on the word of a man. Keith Winslow's opinion was being asked and what he said meant a thousand dollars or more to one man or another. But Otis waited as politely as did my dad.

It wrung my heart the way they were treating him, treating Dad. That low formal talk had been going on all day between the three of 'em. Otis wanted to buy cattle, the code of the country demanded Keith Winslow give 'em a jump, but they didn't like doing business with a man who was selling out. It was written on their faces. It was only poorly concealed in their talk.

"I'd say Haines is about right, Otis," Winslow answered after some thought. "Twenty-three fifty isn't bad either way."

"I'm taking 'em as they come in," Otis pointed out in a flat tone. "They'll lose pounds when I drive 'em over to my grass. But I'll make it twenty-three, Haines."

"Good enough," Dad nodded.

Otis turned to his horse. "I brought the cash," he said a little curtly.

He counted it out—crisp new bills, in big denominations. Neither he nor Dad had to use pencil or paper to figure out what eight hundred and seven times twenty-three totaled. Cattlemen had to figure like that, in their heads.

"I've got a fair string of horses," Dad said as Otis was counting out the money, in hundred-dollar bills. "I'll throw 'em in, all but my pick of three, and make it an even twenty thousand."

Otis nodded and kept right on counting.

"Your remuda, too," murmured Keith Winslow, his eyes peering at Dad. "Looks like you're pulling out, Haines."

My dad smiled faintly. They had been thinking that all day and near busting out their britches waiting for a time to ask him. That time had come.

"No," Dad answered gently. His eyes went from Winslow's face to Otis' and back again. "My kid here has a hankering for the Cimarron country," he explained quietly. "I'm giving him a stake, that's all."

His lips twitched. "I still got my grass," he added. "I got a little in the bank. I may be starting up again—right soon." He took a cigar out of his shirt pocket. "Or I may not," he said slowly.

Otis held out the sheaf of bills. Dad stuck them carelessly into his pants pocket.

"I believe I have a jug in the house, gentlemen," he proposed. "If you wanna set on the porch in the cool . . ."

I held my breath. He had made his explanation. It wasn't what Otis would have done, or Keith Winslow. I wasn't sure how they would react. In their code a man fought for his grass and his cattle to the death, and all who were his by any ties of blood or friendship fought with him to the death also. If they didn't drink, it would mean that they thought . . .

Keith Winslow took off his hat.

"Light, boys," he said gruffly to his hands. "We'll wet our whistles before we mosey on home."

I ducked into the kitchen. Patricia was beating steaks with a heavy wooden mallet. Some of them, we were sure, would stay for supper.

"Did you hear what Dad said?" I demanded excitedly. "Did you know . . . !"

Pat leaned on the table, missing a lick with the mallet. "Yes," she nodded. "He told me this morning before you were up." She sighed, picked up the mallet again.

"He's sending us to the Cimarron . . . to Rich Stewart."

"And he's staying here to . . . !"

"To face Tim Mulloy," she said through tight lips.

"No!" I growled. "I'm sticking with him. You oughta go, this won't be no place for a gal. But me, I'm sticking."

"Don't say that to him, Pete," Pat said in a low voice. "Don't make him remind you that he's the ramrod.

"Besides," she added, "who'd look after me? Could I take the trail for the Cimarron alone?"

"No," I had to concede. "I hadn't thought about that, Pat."

She patted my shoulder again.

# CHAPTER TWO

So there I was on the trail, the magic trail. But my heart wasn't singing as Pat and I rode along at a slow lope. I wasn't thinking so much about what lay at that trail's end as about the man who stayed behind at its beginning, a man who must be lonely by now, if still alive. Two things he had loved, his family and his cattle. He had sold one and he had sent the other away.

We camped that night on the Colorado. Except for the ache inside of me I would have been in hog heaven, for a dozen campfires gleamed around ours, and through the night air floated the low chants of riders making their rounds. The next night we reached the San Gabriel and we had supper with the boys from the Broad B spread near Llano. Except for Pat, I thought as I gorged myself on small thin steaks fried to a wonderful crispness in boiling fat, I could hitch on with an outfit like this. I could talk with 'em to all hours around their campfire instead of having to retire to our lonely camp.

But I didn't complain, of course. Neither did she. Only once did we talk about Dad. That was our first night out; I wondered where he was as we were eating our beans and bacon and cake and Pat said crisply:

"We're not to talk about him, Pete. He said so. If we ever see him again, well and good. If not, no talk. No wondering. No hunting."

I thought back to the last talk Dad had with me. He took me away from Pat, to the corrals where I could barely see his face in the early morning gloom.

"You're going to the Cimarron, Pete," he said perkily. "Rich Stewart is starting a big deal up there. Rich will have a stake. I'm sending a letter with you to Rich telling him what I want him to do. I want him to pick out some good country and buy it now, now before the fences come and the outfits from Texas start moving in. I may join you up there, Pete. I'll try to. But if I don't . . . you're the ramrod 'til I get there. You got Rich to lean on. No boy ever had a finer friend."

"Yes, sir," I gulped. I could agree with that heart and soul. No boy ever had a finer compadre.

"One more thing," he went on sternly as I started to turn off. "The spread in the Cimarron is a new outfit, Pete. No land as yet. No cattle. And no hates, Pete."

I stared at him.

"Promise me," he demanded. "No hates carried over Pete. You'll never ride back to look up a Mulloy?"

"That ain't easy," I mumbled.

"No, it isn't easy," Dad agreed. "But I want your promise, Pete."

I licked my lips. He held out his hand. "Your promise and your hand, Pete," he insisted.

"Dang it, Dad," I protested.

I held out further. "I won't come back and look 'em up," I agreed. "But mebbe . . . what if they come up there . . . or . . ."

"I'm not telling you to run," Dad said sternly. "I'm just asking you not to stir up any dust on an old trail."

"Yes, sir," I agreed, shaking hands with him.

"Good boy, Pete," he murmured. It still wasn't daylight but I could see his lips part in a faint smile.

After that first night Patricia and I never mentioned him.

It was dull business, riding the trail with a girl. We couldn't run our horses; she was sidesaddle and the best we could do was a lope. I could do a little hunting while she built a fire and put coffee on to boil but not much; I didn't dare get too far away from camp. A girl like her had to be looked after all the time.

But she did her best, I'll grant that. She sang around the fire at night and taught me songs and even tried to coach me on carrying a tune. She was up early and when we stopped at towns she filled her saddlebags with canned goods and the night I dropped a deer we had a feast fit for a king. She barbecued it with onions and a sauce made of canned tomatoes and some kind of herbs and melted fat and I ate on a cold haunch all the next day. It was the best venison ham I ever tasted.

I guess the main gripe I had was the time she took with her hair every morning; she wouldn't take the trail 'til it was done up right and sometimes it was eight o'clock before we were riding. That, plus stopping early, and riding slowly, made us forever reaching the Red.

I had been itching for days to get that far, and to see Doan's. Every outfit I had ever talked with had crossed at Doan's. I don't know what I expected to see, but it was something out of the ordinary. And, when we got there, there was only a handful of frame houses and this low long store where a dozen men loafed around pickle barrels and over checker games.

Pat bought groceries, of course. It was still mid-afternoon and we figured on swimming the river and making some miles into the Cimarron before night. She was getting to be about as eager as I was to get on up the trail.

The guy Doan who had built the store was a baldheaded little chap who didn't talk much but did a lot of looking. After Pat had bought a few things and paid him, Doan said:

"You'd be Miss Patricia Haines, wouldn't you?"

She nodded, eyes widening in surprise. I stepped close to her. How did this guy Doan know that?

He turned to a stack of letters behind the counter. "Letter for you," he said.

Pat showed it to me. The address was in Dad's handwriting.

She jerked it open then and there and I read it over her shoulder. Our quick hopes fell when, in the first paragraph, we saw that he had written the letter the day before we had left. It was a long letter. Part of it was to me marked "private" and part to Pat.

In it he had written some things he had been unable to say to us face to face.

Pat didn't finish hers before she turned to me and said, "Let's go."

I knew why she was in such a hurry. So was I.

We didn't want to go on reading that letter there before those men at Doan's. For we couldn't keep from crying as we read it.

They had talked about Indians at Doan's and that night Pat and I split guard duty. We put out our fire just as soon as we had warmed our beans and bacon and we took turns staying awake. But the only Indians we saw were on a hill a mile or more away and, if they saw us at all, they didn't show it.

Though our horses were getting gaunt, we started riding faster and longer. And, four days away from Doan's, we came to the town of Cimarron.

It was a mushroom place. The corrals had been newly built, as had the big gaudy saloon and the two-story frame building that advertised itself as a hotel. Some of the other houses might have been there a year or more; they had never been painted and lumber can get to look old mighty fast. There was a single dusty street, a long flat-roofed building that had signs all over its front—"post office," "store," "rifles and shells," tobacco signs.

Like at Doan's, I was disappointed.

"Shucks," I told Pat, "this ain't any different from Cotulla."

She nodded. I could tell she was disappointed, too. But I think hers was more because we hadn't seen hide nor hair of Rich Stewart, nor heard of him. Dad had written Rich a letter the same day he had dispatched the missive to us at Doan's. Rich was sure to have gotten it. But we got only blank questioning looks as we rode down the street toward the hotel. Not only was Rich not there to meet us but nobody had been posted that we were coming.

I finally pulled up and asked a lanky mustached man if he knew where we could find Rich Stewart.

"He ain't in town," I was told. Meanwhile curious eyes surveyed Pat and me from head to toe. "Reckon if anybody knows about him, it would be Lula Belle."

"Where can I find her?" I demanded. I guess I was a little self-conscious before those curious looks.

"See that saloon? Ride down there, light, walk inside and ask for Lula Belle."

Pat and I turned our horses around; we had ridden past the saloon a block or more. I frowned as we pulled up before the hitching rail, which was gilted like everything else about the front of the building.

"Reckon I'd better go in by myself," I said.

"I guess," she answered faintly.

I swung out of the saddle, hitched my belt and walked inside. I had been in saloons, yes, like Yancey's and the Buckhorn at San Antonio, but never a place like this. There was a long gleaming bar and a polished dance floor and tables sitting around and a small stage and, behind the dance floor, a roulette wheel. I had heard the trail hands talk about the honkey-tonks in Kansas. Nothing there, I thought, could hold a candle to this. The bartender wore a white coat and there were girls sitting at the tables with the few customers and they wore low-cut costumes that broke off above their knees like the trail men had said.

While I stood there gawking a woman left one of the tables and walked toward me. She had on a full-length dress unlike most of the others but it clung to her tight and was low in front and she was a full-breasted woman anyhow and I turned red from what I was suddenly thinking. She was pretty, though she had on too much paint and powder. I had never seen a dress as fine as hers, of a gold-like material almost the same shade as her hair. And her bracelets jingled as she walked toward me. She must have been wearing a half dozen.

"We can't serve you, friend," she told me with a smile. "You're a little young."

She had a nice smile. And nice eyes. As soon as she spoke I wasn't afraid of her any more.

"I don't want to be served," I answered quickly. "I want to ask about Rich Stewart."

"What about him?"

"Where is he?"

"At his camp, I'm sure. It's about twelve miles from here, on the edge of the reservation."

Meanwhile she was studying me from under her heavy lashes.

"I think," she smiled, holding out her hand suddenly, "you are Pete Haines. Right?"

"Right," I said.

"How did you know?" I demanded.

"Rich has told everybody in Cimarron about his compadre in Texas," she said, her eyes twinkling. She took my arm and turned me toward the bar. "The house rules are off," she smiled. "You can be served here any time, friend. I know you're no average sixteen-year-old."

I looked my astonishment. Hell's hatoot, this woman even knew how old I was!

"Wet your whistle with something easy," she proposed, "and tell me how you moseyed up this far."

"I don't believe I want a drink," I hesitated. "Besides, my sister is waiting out there. I'd like to get us a place to stay and to send word . . ."

"Your sister is here! Patricia!"

"Yes. Outside. She didn't . . ." I caught myself just in time; I was going to say that she didn't come into places like this.

The woman was frowning.

"We wrote a letter to Rich," I explained. "Dad did, I mean. Dad wrote him that we were selling out our stock and Patricia and I . . ."

"Rich hasn't been in town for a couple of weeks," the honkey-tonk woman explained. "He didn't know about it. The letter got here. I'm holding it for him.

"How long are you going to stay?" she asked in the next breath.

"Why, gosh," I answered, "we're here for good."

"You're settling here!" she exclaimed. "At Cimarron?"

"Sure," I nodded. Then, struck with a sudden horrible thought: "Unless Rich doesn't want us."

She laughed softly and squeezed my arm. "Don't give that another thought, friend," she assured me. "Rich is plumb loco over the both of you. As soon as he knows you're here he'll ride in hell-for-breakfast."

She turned around and waved to a one-eyed man who had a wide white scar on his left cheek.

"Squint," she ordered, "ride out to Rich's camp and tell him to come in today, that he has visitors."

Squint obeyed quickly. Evidently this voluptuous woman owned the place.

She gave another order. She sent a tall well-dressed man to the hotel.

"Tell Luke to fix up his best rooms for Pete and his sister," she ordered. "Tell him it is Rich's sweetheart from Texas and her brother."

The door was open; I could see that Patricia was taking all of this in. This honkey-tonk woman turned and she looked out at Patricia.

"Your sister is pretty," she murmured. "She is as pretty as Rich said she was."

"Much obliged," I said awkwardly. "We'll mosey on down to the hotel."

She nodded and held out her hand.

"My name is Lula Belle, Pete," she said gently. "Rich and I have known each other a long time. There is nobody I think more of. A compadre of his is a compadre of mine."

"Much obliged," I said. I wanted to only touch

her hand but she wouldn't have it so; she caught mine and held it tight a moment.

As soon as I could get free I went back to Patricia. The well-dressed man—he had on white broadcloth and black linen—was already well down the street.

"We'll go on to the hotel," I told Pat. "Rich hasn't been in town and hasn't got Dad's letter. That man," and I motioned down the street, "is going to fix us up with rooms at the hotel. A rider has gone out to Rich's camp to tell him to come in."

"That woman," Patricia said coldly, "who is she?"

"Name is Lula Belle." I looked up at the front of the saloon. It was named the Lula Belle. "Reckon she owns the place."

"She certainly seems to be running things around here," Pat observed. "Did she know Rich?"

I sighed. "She seems to know him real well," I had to admit.

We rode on in silence.

The man who owned the hotel was named Luke Martin. He made a to-do over us.

"If I'd knowed you were coming, Miss Haines," he told my sister, "I would have been ready for you. My wife is putting clean blankets on the beds. I've given you our southeast room, the coolest in the place. I'll get the beds out of the room next to it in the morning and fix you up a sitting room with chairs and books and a piano. And I know you're tired, I'll bring up a tub of hot water."

"Thank you," Pat answered wearily. It seemed to me her lips were a little tight as we went upstairs.

Mr. Martin followed us. "Supper is about six," he chattered on. "I'll send up a table and you can eat in your room if you don't feel like coming downstairs."

"We'll come down, thanks," my sister answered in the same aloof fashion.

The hotel man brought us up a pitcher of cool water and offered lemonade, which Patricia declined. As the door closed behind Luke Martin I grinned:

"They know who Rich is in this country, don't they?"

"Yes," Pat agreed.

She sank down on the bed. Here Luke came back with a tub of hot water.

I eyed it longingly, and surprised myself by requesting the same service.

"You mean," Pat gasped, "you'll take a bath voluntarily!"

"And comb my hair," I grinned.

I soaked awhile in the suds, then put on my Sunday suit. I peeped into Pat's room when she didn't answer my call and saw she was sleeping like the dead. She had stood the ride well, better than I had thought she could. I wasn't surprised that she was out like a log. I suppose she had never ridden over five miles in any one stretch until we started for the Cimarron.

Downstairs Luke greeted me warmly. "Feeling better, ain't you?" he grinned, noticing how clean and spruced-up I was.

"Quite a ride," I said carelessly.

He reached under his desk top and brought out a ledger. "Didn't bother you with it while ago," he said, "but reckon you'd better register."

I took the stub-pointed pencil and started to write my name and Pat's on the soiled paper. But I wrote only "Pe" when the pencil fell from my hand.

There, on the line above the one I had started to write on, in a shaky scrawl, was written:

"Tim Mulloy, Texas."

And above that, in the same handwriting:

"Jeb Mulloy, Texas."

Luke Martin noticed my agitation. "Reckon they're friends of yours. They asked if I had seen you when they signed up."

"No," I said faintly, "they're not friends of ours."

I didn't explain further. I didn't even write our names on the register. Luke looked at me a moment, then stuck the book back under the desk without another word.

"If you need help, son," he said quietly, "old Luke is your man. Rich Stewart set me up here."

"Thanks," I said helplessly.

I didn't know what to do. Tim Mulloy and his cousin in Cimarron! They must have been only an hour or so behind us on the trail. They were bound to be following us, for a Mulloy would have no business here. What had happened back in Cotulla? Was Dad killed? Had Mulloy shot him down and then immediately taken up the chase of the last living Haines? They could have left a couple of days after us, I reflected, and still nearly caught us before we got to Cimarron. We were that slow on the trail. I shivered as I thought of our near escape. What would we have done if we had heard hoof beats behind and turned to find Tim Mulloy and his ugly cousin thundering down upon us!

What was I to do now? I could guess that they were at the saloon washing the trail dust out of their throats with whiskey. If they had come this far after me, they would surely shoot on sight.

I had left my gun in my room. I turned and started upstairs for it. Then I heard a clatter of hoofs outside and a rider swung out of his saddle in front of the hotel. I knew the chestnut horse before I knew the man.

"Rich!" I yelled, near bursting the door open in my eagerness.

He was sweaty and covered with a white

chalky dust but there was that quick grin and that flash in his eyes and there was his cheery "glad to see you, partner" and then his arm around my shoulders, tight, reassuring. I laid my head against his sweaty-smelling shirt for a moment. Then suddenly I had to laugh.

    I had wanted it. So had Dad. Pride had kept Dad from sending for him, though he had grinned at the idea. Damn their souls, I thought, the Mulloys have ridden into it, ridden right into Rich Stewart.

# CHAPTER THREE

We sat on the hotel steps and he listened with his hat pulled down low over his eyes. He wore a smaller brimmed hat than most men, and a softer one; the rains had soaked it and it flopped down low over his ears and his forehead.

"I didn't get the letter," he said when I slowed up. "Reckon it's at Lula Belle's."

"She said it was."

"I remember Tim," he mused. "Always thought he was a pretty square hombre. This Jeb, where did he come from?"

I told him what I knew about Jeb Mulloy, including the six notches on Jeb's gun.

"But I'll betcha that you can drill him before he makes his draw," I said quickly. I had justification for that loyalty. I had never seen him in a fight, nor had anyone in the Frio, but trail drivers had brought back yarns of Rich Stewart and his gunplay.

"Never can tell about that," he murmured.

He rolled a cigarette with a slow deliberate motion. He started to speak once, then changed his mind. Then a group of riders coming down the road caught his attention. Also mine, for they were all soldiers. Dust almost hid the blue color of their uniforms and all except their leader slouched in their saddles with fatigue. That leader wore a black hat and had a dark beard touched here and there with gray. They came on to the hotel, where the leader pulled up and said in a crisp voice:

"Lieutenant Fairchild, I suggest you pitch camp down by the creek."

He said it like it was spelled "crick." A young man who had been riding a half pace behind the leader saluted and said: "Yes, General."

"You will be my guest at dinner," went on the bearded man.

I watched him with wide eyes as he stiffly dismounted. Golly Moses, a general! I turned to Rich. There was no change of expression on his face, but I sensed his tenseness.

The General came towards us with short quick steps. He started by us without a word, then stopped suddenly. He seemed to bend over a little and peer at Rich, who sat not over six feet from him.

"Mr. Stewart?" he barked. That was his voice, a bark.

Rich came slowly to his feet. "Howdy, General," he drawled.

Rich towered over him by half a head but the General was broader, and there was something about the man in the blue tunic that made him seem bigger than he actually was.

"Were you notified about the hearing, sir?" the General demanded.

"Yes, General."

"You didn't answer my note," snapped the officer.

"Got it out at camp, General," Rich explained in his slow voice. "Couldn't get off an answer."

Of course he couldn't, I thought. Someone would have had to write such a message for him. And probably there wasn't a rider in his outfit who could draft a decent letter.

The General seemed disgruntled. His attitude showed that he was not accustomed to having his messages go unanswered. Then, with a clicking of his teeth, he said snappishly:

"Very well, Mr. Stewart. We'll see you in the morning at nine o'clock."

"Yes, General," Rich agreed.

The officer was barely inside the hotel when I whispered to Rich: "General who?"

"Sheridan."

"General Sheridan!" I gasped.

I had heard of him. What Texan hadn't?

"Sheridan," Rich said with a quick grin. "You thought he'd be wearing horns, didn't you?"

"Something like that," I agreed. "He doesn't look much . . ."

"He's a tough one," Rich said as I groped for words.

He stood up. "Got a gun upstairs?" he murmured.

"Yes."

"Better strap it on," he advised grimly. "I need a drink. The Mulloys might be in the saloon."

I hesitated. "Dad said that . . ." I started to protest.

Rich cut me short. "Reckon I can guess what your dad said. I had a respect for him as everybody knows. But the way I see it, I'm ramrodding this outfit now. My way might be different from what your dad thought."

I stared at him. "Get your gun," he repeated.

I wobbled a little as I went up the stairs and down again. I was scared, of course. I had never aimed that gun at a human being. I had practiced a draw some, on the sly, but I knew I was slow and, besides, I was sure my fingers would be all thumbs when I faced a Mulloy.

He nodded when I rejoined him on the steps.

"The only way I know to handle trouble is to go and meet it, Pete," he explained as we walked along.

"I don't mind," I said, trying to be as cool as he was.

He didn't seem to be in a hurry. Our heels scuffed a low waltz-like rhythm on the boardwalk as we clomped along. It was a couple of blocks. Rich spoke to some men coming in the opposite direction.

"Good luck tomorrow, hombre," one of them called after him.

I guess I must have calmed down some as we

walked, because I began to notice what was in the stores as we passed. I caught Rich's arm as we passed an open door.

"What's that place?" I asked. I had noticed machinery inside.

"Newspaper office," he grunted. "We got everything in Cimarron, including a newspaper publisher."

Then we were in front of the saloon and everything inside of me was hollow again.

Rich stepped quickly through the swinging door with me at his heels. I pointed my shoulders like he did, holding my right hand low. And I made sure I wasn't hiding behind his body. I wasn't hiding from any Mulloy.

One swift glance told me neither Mulloy was in the saloon. I sighed and not from relief. The moment must come when I had to face them and I was prepared for it then.

The woman called Lula Belle came quickly toward us. A sixteen-year-old might not know much about love, but I could tell right off what she thought about Rich Stewart. He slipped his arm around her careless-like and turned to me.

"What do you think of him, Lula Belle?"

"The saltiest cowhand to come out of Texas yet," she responded. "Come on, Rich, I'll buy a drink while you get your mail."

We sat at a corner table. I noticed that Lula Belle opened his letters as if used to doing it.

One was from Hy Moran of Ben Ficklin, Texas. He would deliver three thousand head of young stuff by September 1. Another was from General Philip Sheridan. "Dear Mr. Stewart: A committee of residents of the town of Cimarron this morning presented a petition that your activities . . ."

I listened to her drone through the official language. Some men, led by a Martin Champion, were claiming that his lease of grazing land from the Arapaho Indians would create unrest among the red men and lead to Indian outrages. An agent from the Arapaho reservation, a man named Jenson, argued that the Indians could not be controlled if they had a source of revenue other than the government. The sum and total of the complaints was that General Sheridan invited Mr. Stewart to present his remarks in person or by letter.

"You got his notice about the hearing in the morning?" Lula Belle stopped reading to ask.

He nodded.

"They're after you, Rich," she said gravely. "That Scot—Cameron, isn't it?—is bringing in new families. They want to settle on your land south of the reservation."

"So I heard," he shrugged. "Their talk doesn't make sense. The Indians are threatening, they say in one breath. In the next they want to settle their families right on the edge of the reservation. Who'd protect the families?"

"That's Champion's doings," Lula Belle explained. "He says his newspaper will be out next week, Rich."

"What's this hearing about?" I demanded. I had been kept in the dark long enough.

"I got a lease with the Arapaho Indians," Rich said. "My camp is on my own land—government lease—but I'm running stock on the Indians' grass. I'm paying 'em in cash instead of supplies. The Indian agent is hollering his head off because he is afraid the Arapahos will scorn the reservation supplies and buy their own. That way he wouldn't get to steal from 'em. This Champion Lula Belle talks about—he's from the East. I can't figure whether he's a four-flusher or not. He has got a notion of starting a newspaper and getting a railroad here and organizing the territory into a state. There's a cattleman named Bob Purdy who is plumb mad because the Arapahos wouldn't make a deal with him. There are some nesters who want to homestead on the land I've leased from the government. They have petitioned Washington not to renew my lease, which comes up next month. But they know I'll get it renewed unless this General Sheridan orders it cancelled as a military necessity. That's the only chance they got."

I thought of Sheridan's bearded countenance and remembered the things I had heard about him in Texas.

"Seems like you got enough troubles," I sighed, "without us coming in on top of you."

I saw him go tense and I knew without looking up that the Mulloys were walking into the saloon.

I slowly turned my head. There they were standing against the bar. Tim's face was darker than ever. There was kind of a loose grin on Jeb Mulloy's lips. Probably, I thought, he was hankering to put another notch on his gun handle.

They saw me. They stood there staring at me. Then Tim Mulloy walked toward me.

I came to my feet but there was Rich in front of me. There was Rich moving out to meet Mulloy. I turned my attention upon Jeb. Rich could handle Tim, or either of them. It was up to me to see they didn't gang him.

Tim stopped. He knew Rich. He knew also—I could tell it by the sudden tightening of his lips—that Rich Stewart was something with a six-gun.

"Howdy, Mulloy," drawled Rich. "Seems kind of funny to run into you this far North."

"I was trailing the button there," Tim answered, nodding toward me. "I got some business with him."

"Don't believe," Rich murmured, "I'd make a move toward him if I were you, Mulloy. I'm gonna marry his sister if you never heard. Even if it weren't for that, he'd be a compadre of mine."

"I got nothing against the button," Tim Mulloy said harshly. "He's too young for a man's fight.

But I figger his dad will show up around here sooner or later. It's Frank Haines I'm after, Stewart."

My heart leaped. Then Dad was alive!

Rich frowned. I could understand his hesitation. In his code a man had the right to challenge another.

"Don't reckon Frank is coming up this far, Mulloy," he pointed out. "Last word I had from him he was figuring on staying in Texas."

"That was his bluff," snarled Mulloy. "He sent his boy and his gal away. He waited 'til they were plumb gone. Then he bushwhacked my boy and made a getaway himself."

Rich shot a quick glance at me. I was staring at Mulloy as if I couldn't believe what the thin black-eyed man was saying. His boy bushwhacked! Then Skip must . . .

"Killed not a mile from the house," Tim said bitterly, sensing the inquiry in my look. "I don't blame the button there, Stewart. But I'm sticking around. And when Frank Haines shows up here . . ."

"Haines didn't bushwhack your boy, Mulloy," Rich said quietly. "Your folks and his have had a hate on a long time. But neither of you ever sunk to that."

"We never did," Mulloy vowed. "We fought in the open and we always sent 'em word we were coming. But Frank Haines was never a fighting man. Never wore a gun at all. Mebbe he thought Skip was me; we were about the same size and build even if he was only a button."

"He didn't bushwhack him, Mulloy," Rich repeated.

"He stayed there to fight you," I put in.

Rich hitched his belt. It was a favorite gesture of his just before having something to say.

"Listen to me, Mulloy," he said coldly. "This is a different country from Texas. This is *my* country. Pete Haines and his sister are mine to look after. I can do it. I'll take you on any minute you say, you and that gimp-eyed cousin both. And you know what I'll do to you."

It was a haughty thing to say. It was a cruel thing. For the flash in Tim Mulloy's eyes, the tightening of Tim Mulloy's lips, plainly showed that Mulloy was well aware of Rich Stewart's reputation as a gunman. It would no more be a fair fight than a duel between my father and Tim would have been.

"You've trailed 'em to the Cimarron," went on Stewart. "*Bueno.* Leave 'em here. Get back to Texas, to your own country."

"You're a tough hombre, Stewart," Tim said slowly. "I'm not grabbing leather with you."

A faint smile curved Stewart's lips. I suppose a man could no more help feeling a tinge of pride about such a compliment than if he had been praised for his riding, his cattle judgment, or his looks.

"But," continued Mulloy, "there are other ways to skin a cat. When Frank Haines bushwhacked my boy, he let down the bars. Anything goes."

"Call the turn," Rich shrugged. "I got the biggest outfit in this country, Mulloy. I got a dozen men riding for me who can outshoot anything you ever saw in the Frio. If you get any bushwhacking notions . . . remember that. I'll leave word with 'em that if anything happens to me, or to my compadre here, that a certain gent named Mulloy ain't to get back to Texas."

"I'll remember that," Tim nodded. "Remember something yourself, Stewart. Remember there is more than one way to skin a cat."

With that he turned back to the bar. He and his cousin had a drink together, holding their backs to us, not even looking at us in the mirror.

I felt faint inside. Skip Mulloy bushwhacked! Dad on the run! Tim and Jeb Mulloy waiting for him to show up in Cimarron.

"He won't come here," Rich told me gently. "Frank Haines will watch his back trail. He knew days ago what the Mulloys were up to."

"Rich," I appealed, "you know Dad didn't bushwhack Skip, don't you?"

"Sure as I know I'm sitting here," he declared.

Lula Belle came back to our table. The glitter

of her gown sparkled in the glow from the oil lamps.

"The gentlemen there," she said, nodding toward the Mulloys, "are peeved about something."

"A feud," Rich shrugged. "Me and Pete might have to wipe out the whole bunch some day."

"Seems to me," Lula Belle said, and I thought her voice was a little sour, "you can stir up more trouble than any other dozen men I know. Ain't you got enough on your hands with this hearing and with these nesters?"

"This one," Rich answered with a faint grin, "I didn't ask for." Then, after a look at me: "But I'm tickled pink to take it on."

A bearded man in blue flannel shirt and overrun boots came into the saloon and shuffled quickly to our table.

"A herd is coming in, Rich!" he announced. "I think it's from Hy Moran."

"It would be," grunted Rich. "Hy is always early. Runs the flesh off his cows on the trail."

"The corrals aren't ready," Lula Belle pointed out. "If there are three thousand head . . ."

"We'll drive 'em straight onto the reservation," he said.

"What about the hearing?"

Rich nodded. "We'll get our lease upheld. Pecos, tell who's in charge to bed the cows down outside of town. The hearing oughta be over by noon. Then we'll trail 'em on to the reservation. Better get the boys in town ready to take over."

"In case General Sheridan turns his thumbs down," Lula Belle murmured, "which he is pretty apt to do, Mister Stewart has three thousand head of Texas cattle that he can't feed. Then what?"

Rich patted her shoulder. "You worry too much, Lula Belle," he said lightly. "It ain't good for your complexion."

"Somebody in this outfit has gotta worry," she pointed out.

Rich turned to me and proposed we walk back to the hotel. "I got a hankering to see that sister of yours," he grinned.

I nodded. We walked past the Mulloys without a sidewise look. It gave me an eerie feeling to know they were looking into our backs and I was a-tremble until we reached the board sidewalk.

Then I shot a questioning look at my compadre. "This Lula Belle," I said, "she acts like she has something to say about your outfit."

"She does," Rich nodded. "She's put up some of the money."

I didn't like that. Nor, I thought swiftly, would Patricia. Partners with a honkey-tonk woman!

"She's all wool and a yard wide, pardner," Rich went on. "As soon as this fool hearing is over, I wanna get things better organized. You can gimme a jump with what you've learned in school. I got cattle coming up the trail all summer and fall. I'll need an office here, and papers. I'm gonna appoint you vice-president and business manager of the Cimarron Cattle Company, pardner. I figure on you paying for the stuff as it comes and ordering all supplies."

"Gosh, Rich," I faltered, "it takes a smart man to do all that. And, Golly Moses, I'm just . . ."

His hand fell on my shoulder. "You're Frank Haines' kid," he said quietly. "You'll learn plumb quick what you don't know already."

We reached the hotel. I stopped.

"Believe I'll saunter around a little," I suggested. "You go on up. Pat is sure to be awake by now."

His grin rewarded me for my understanding.

"You may be a button," he said, "but you ain't so thick between the ears. See you at supper, Petey."

# CHAPTER FOUR

The hearing was set for Foley's store at nine o'clock. It was straight up eight when General Sheridan clomped downstairs and ordered his breakfast. He didn't like his eggs fried but ordered medium soft-boiled. He wanted biscuits. He sat straight as a rod and gave his orders and the hotel man fell all over himself running to obey 'em.

Rich wasn't around when Pat and I came down, a little after seven. I told her what I knew about the hearing; he hadn't mentioned it to her the night before. Nor had he said anything about Tim Mulloy and the word Tim had brought from Texas, that Skip Mulloy had been bushwhacked and Dad was on the dodge. I didn't tell her about that. I'll give her a few days to get over the trip, I thought, before worrying her with that.

She left me right after breakfast to see if there were any women's clothes at Foley's. She had brought only one nice dress from the Frio country; she had that on.

"You'd better get some things yourself, Pete," she advised.

I shook my head. I couldn't be worried about clothes, not with that hearing coming up. Rich had sunk a lot of money in his cattle company already. I had tried to tell it to Pat so it would make sense but she didn't have cattle sabbe. This Arapaho country grass was high and rich. The Cimarron Cattle Company was buying range stock from Texas, throwing it on the virgin range, and the profit was what weight the cows would gain. It was a big deal. Rich could handle maybe forty thousand head a year. He stood to gain five bucks a head if the grass held out. It would be there a year or two anyhow. And his lease was for two years.

It was easy to see why a woman like Lula Belle would be interested. I was wondering how to suggest to Patricia that we sink the twenty thousand Dad had raised for us in the Cimarron deal. The payoff would be plenty.

There was a tenseness about this town of Cimarron in the early hours of that morning. I moseyed by the building where Rich said they were going to print a newspaper and there were a dozen horses hitched in front and inside as many men were poring over papers. By eight o'clock there was a crowd at Lula Belle's. Mostly they were cowhands, some of 'em from the Texas herd that was bedded down outside of town. I met Hy Moran himself; he was hollering all over the place for Rich Stewart to show his face.

"That two-bit four-flushing bronk peeler," he roared. "I rode this far just to drink him under the table and he ain't got the guts to show up."

He was near loopity already, Hy was. He roared out his denunciations of those challenging Rich's lease.

"Them damned Kansas lawyers and them newspaper guys! They ruined every trail town in Kansas. Used to be you could have good times in Dodge. Or Ellsworth. Now they're tamed down. We can bring our cattle in there if we act real sweet and don't make any noise. But Lula Belle there, she always had a good place. Plenty of us Texans will bring our cattle to the town where Lula Belle is."

She was wearing a silvery sort of gown this morning, of a different color and texture from the other but showing about as much of her shoulders and the first firm swell of her breasts. She was talking to some men at the bar when Hy roared out his praise; she walked over to his table, kissed his bald head and motioned to the barkeep to bring one on the house.

Hy hugged her.

"Dang it, Lula Belle," complained the Texas cattleman, "you're always teasing a man. Some of these days I'm gonna hawg-tie you, throw you across my saddle and carry you back to Texas."

She laughed and kissed his temple again.

The Mulloys came in. Tim stood at the end of the bar watching everything through his narrow eyelids. Jeb roamed around the place a little, mixing with the Texas hands. Some of the soldiers trooped in and drank, standing away from the cowmen. I watched them curiously. There had been no Yankee troopers in Texas in my lifetime, but I had heard tales about them. Not any of these soldiers were Negroes. I wondered if the U. S. Government had learned at last the folly of garrisoning stations in the Southwest with colored troops.

About eight-thirty the men I had seen in the newspaper office came in for a quick one before the hearing. Most of them were dressed up like preachers or lawyers, in linen and broadcloth, wearing black hats. They talked to each other in low excited voices. They were served, but I noticed that neither Lula Belle nor the two flimsily clad girls on hand for this early morning rush of business had anything to do with 'em. The attitude of this saloon toward the soldiers and the black-and-white dressed men was clear. They could pay their money and get their drinks but the management of the place wanted it to be a hangout for Rich Stewart and his friends. Even if Lula Belle's money hadn't been behind Rich, I mused, it would have been so. It was the cattlemen coming up the trail, the Hy Morans, who made such a saloon pay.

I saw Pat pass outside and I overtook her and suggested we go back to Foley's and get a seat for the hearing. She had several packages; she had found one or two dresses she liked.

"They're awfully daring, Pete," she smiled. It was almost a giggle. She touched her breast. "They don't seem to wear *anything* up here," she complained.

"They sure don't," I agreed, thinking about Lula Belle.

General Sheridan was coming from the hotel with short quick steps, looking neither to the right nor to the left of him.

"We'd better hurry," I said.

Foley was clearing out barrels of stuff from the center of his store, providing an open space about twenty by fifteen for the hearing. I took a board and fixed us up a bench in the back by laying it across two kegs. Now the crowd was gathering. The group of men I had noticed in the newspaper office, who had made a quick visit to the saloon, came in first. I heard scuffling sounds outside and turned to see bearded faces peering through the windows. They were Rich Stewart's riders, and the men from Hy Moran's outfit.

I overheard some of the talk with Sheridan. At least two of the men, I realized, were lawyers. They had come clear from Kansas City to plead the causes of their clients. I sighed. Rich wouldn't think to hire a lawyer. With it nearly nine, with General Sheridan looking at his gold-cased watch every now and then, Rich wasn't even here himself.

One of the lawyers had a booming voice and I

could hear snatches of his talk: "Here to defend the rights of the common citizen," "here to plead justice for all, not favoritism for a few." They made much over Sheridan. "General, we are pleased beyond words that you are conducting this hearing yourself." "General, I was almost under you in the war. I petitioned for a transfer and . . ." I swore softly. Rich wouldn't butter up the man like that, not even if he lost his lease. And Sheridan seemed to like it.

"Rich should have hired somebody like that to speak for him," I whispered to Pat.

She nodded.

Sheridan turned away from his flatterers for a moment. "Is Mr. Stewart here?" he asked in a loud voice.

There was no answer. "It is straight up nine," grunted the General. "Mr. Stewart should be here."

I could see the triumphant looks exchanged between the lawyers. Rich was at a psychological disadvantage already. Sheridan obviously was a man who didn't like to be kept waiting.

"Where in the world is Rich?" Pat whispered.

I shook my head. I hadn't seen him all morning.

Then, over the hum of voices, came the clatter of hoofs outside. I turned to the window. There he was, rolling out of his saddle, quickly tethering the sweaty chestnut, coming up the walk now with long quick strides.

I groaned. He hadn't even bothered to change clothes. He stood there in stained shirt and denim pants. His boots were scuffed and overrun at the heels. His faded hat flopped down over his forehead.

"If you're ready, Mr. Stewart," Sheridan said crisply, "we'll begin the hearing."

Rich nodded. "Shoot," he said. He looked around for a place to sit. There was none left. He leaned against the wall and slowly rolled a cigarette.

Sheridan called the hearing to order. The first speaker was the booming-voice man from Kansas City, a lawyer named Pettigrew. He attacked the legality of Rich Stewart's lease with the Arapaho Indians. How could a ward of the government execute a legal instrument, he argued, without the consent of that government's representative who was General Sheridan himself? Was the alleged lease a legal document? Had it been notarized? Were the Indian chieftains who were alleged to have signed the document officially authorized to act for the tribe?

"My other colleagues," he said, "will present other objections to the approval of such a lease. I merely attack its legality. I challenge Mr. Stewart to produce his lease at this moment. Let us appraise the document and determine its legal character."

He pointed his finger accusingly at Rich.

He waited. When Rich calmly smoked on his cigarette, giving no indication that he had heard Pettigrew's challenge, the lawyer turned appealingly to General Sheridan.

"Do you have the document with you, Mr. Stewart?" the officer demanded.

"Yes, sir," Rich answered at once.

"Mr. Pettigrew would like to examine it," Sheridan said impatiently.

Rich took a final puff on his cigarette, crushed it under his heel, then answered slowly: "He's speaking for the other side, General. Reckon it's my right to show the lease in my own good time."

Sheridan's mouth tightened. "You are right, sir," he conceded. His voice was almost a bark.

Pettigrew conceded the point. His manner plainly showed that Rich Stewart's refusal to exhibit his document with the Arapahos indicated that the lease was not in order.

Other speakers followed him. One, Pettigrew's partner, droned through several case histories of leases made by individuals with Indians.

Then the Arapaho agent, a shrewd-eyed man named Walt Jenson, testified. He declared that such leases brought only trouble.

"We hold one axe over the Indians' heads," he said, "and that's food. If they go on a warpath, they don't get rations issued at the agency. Mr. Stewart proposes to pay the Arapahos in cash. That will make them independent of the agency for at least a part of the year. During those months they will be free to prowl and raid. The proper way to handle any lease with the Indians is to have the lessee pay over his money to the agency and let the agent spend it for supplies which will be issued to the Indians from time to time, as they are needed. The red man is both a child and a glutton. He should not be trusted to spend his money as he sees fit."

Jenson sat down. General Sheridan turned to Rich.

"Any questions, Mr. Stewart?"

"Only one, General."

"You may ask it of Mr. Jenson," Sheridan said as Rich hesitated.

"No point of asking him," Stewart answered. "*You* can answer it, General. The Arapahos leased part of their land last year under the terms Mr. Jenson mentioned. Mr. Jenson handled the money, bought the supplies, issued them to the Arapahos. But the Arapahos didn't like it much. Did they, General?"

"How would I know, man?" Sheridan snapped.

"You spent a good part of your time chasing 'em down," shrugged Rich. "I figured you would remember."

"I'm not testifying," the General said crossly.

"Nope," agreed Rich. "But you're doing the deciding."

Sheridan glared a moment, then motioned

to Pettigrew, who was apparently ramrodding the plaintiff's cause. Pettigrew said that Martin Champion, who would soon publish a newspaper in Cimarron, would speak next. Champion stood up, and he was the stocky-looking man with the bright blue eyes that I had decided was the best of the bunch. Before he could start talking there was a stir at the door and in stepped the Mulloys. They looked around for a perch, saw none, and moved back against the door.

Pat's voice was a low frightened hiss in my ear. "What are they doing here?" she demanded. I squeezed her hand.

"Tell you about it later," I promised.

Champion was talking now. He had a better voice even than the Kansas City lawyer. He told General Sheridan that Cimarron was a town in the making. Homesteaders were waiting to settle in the open country south of the Arapaho reservation if the General would only nullify Rich Stewart's lease. It seemed Champion was bringing some of the settlers out there himself with his Cimarron Land Company. There were, he declared, thirty families of Scots who had emigrated from Kentucky.

"They are fine citizens," he declared. "They helped to build one great state. They helped to establish one frontier. They want to build homes, schools, churches. They want to advertise in a newspaper. What does Mr. Stewart propose to do? He proposes to ally himself with a honkey-tonk woman."

Rich had begun to roll another cigarette. The tobacco spilled to the floor and the paper fluttered away from his fingers. I felt Pat stiffen at my side.

"For Mr. Stewart's purpose," continued this Martin Champion, "this must be a wide-open town. The woman Lula Belle, famous in Kansas towns, has built an ornate saloon and has appealed to Texas cattlemen to bring their herds to Cimarron, where a good spree awaits a man at the end of the drive. Mr. Stewart and this woman, Lula Belle, are seeking to build here a replica of what Dodge City was, and Abilene, and Ellsworth. What is the law in the town of Cimarron today? It is six-gun law. And the sole judge of what is right and wrong is Stewart himself, a man who could wear notches on his gun if it pleased his vanity."

His voice fell off a moment, but he was only pausing for effect, not because of the lack of something to say.

"You, General Sheridan," he urged, "hold the fate of Cimarron in your hands. Mr. Stewart has not presented his lease for our examination. We will concede that he may have such a paper. But Mr. Pettigrew has pointed out the inadequacy of such a document under the letter of the law. Regardless of any merits Mr. Stewart's agreement might hold in a civil court, it is within your province to order such a lease void if you hold that it is contrary to the common good."

He raised his arms and his voice thundered out: "Would you close the door to the spread of American civilization, General Sheridan? Do you hold that the half million acres of rich grazing land and the ten sections of rich farming country Mr. Stewart has under a separate lease should be consigned to one man and the doughty pioneers who have come here from Kentucky and Tennessee turned back? The fate of individuals is not important, General Sheridan, nor are their rights. The future of America is all important. This, sir, is the door to the great west. You, sir, are charged by your government and your people with the task of keeping it open for those worthy intrepid souls who wish to push on!

"There is another thing, General," he said softly. "We have seen in our lifetime the evils of a society that is built upon the ownership of large tracts of land. If these cattlemen are permitted to divide our virgin west into large blocks, we will have a western aristocracy as vicious, as detrimental to our American way, as the Southern slaveholder. . . ."

I saw Rich's face tighten. I saw Sheridan's eyes gleam. Damn Champion anyhow, I thought! He was smart enough to appeal to the General's passionate hate for the South.

"That is all," Champion concluded and turned back to his chair with a triumphant gleam in his eyes. He had spoken well and he knew it.

Sheridan scribbled something on a scratch pad before him with a pencil. Then he motioned to Rich.

"All right, Mr. Stewart," he said crisply.

Rich came forward a few paces. He stood there swaying on his feet as if he didn't know how to begin. I sighed sympathetically. This wasn't his style of fighting, this talk about law and history. He was the son of a nester. My own Dad had loaned him a twenty-dollar goldpiece and a good horse and had advised him to try his luck out of Texas, where his humble origin wouldn't be held against him, where the land wasn't already fenced in but free to those who could take it and hold it. He had been a trail ramrod and a promoter. The stake he had sunk in the Cimarron Cattle Company had been earned the hard way.

"General," Rich said after a moment, drawling his words out, "I plumb enjoyed Mister Champion's little talk. I was getting ready to consider Mister Champion a cheap crook like some of his running mates. But I reckon . . ."

"Mr. Stewart!" Sheridan interrupted with a bark. "Please remember the dignity of this hearing. Please conform your plea to the rules of order."

Rich shook his head. "You want me to have my

say, don't you, General?" he countered. "Well, I gotta say it my way."

Sheridan grunted. I heard Pat's sigh in my ear. I saw the quirk of amusement on Martin Champion's lips. I saw the smile on Tim Mulloy's lean face. It wasn't a pretty smile. It will make it easier for you, I thought. You'd like to see Rich broke and his men scattering.

"Mister Champion's talk kinda appealed to me," Rich went on gently. "I never thought much about the spread of empire and stuff like that. But I've seen it, too. Mebbe I've seen more than he has. I was in Dodge when it was a crossroads town. I saw it die. I was a law in Ellsworth for a spell. The kind of law I stood for ain't the kind of law Mister Champion likes. I don't claim it's the best kind. But it was the only kind there was. It was the only kind there could be."

Something like a smile touched his face. "Things ain't always like we want it out here, General. We have to take it like it is, and do the best we can with it."

I stirred a little. Rich, I thought, was a lot better at this business than I had imagined. He wasn't awed by the lawyers he faced, nor by the stars on Sheridan's shoulders. But that was like him, I mused. Had he ever been awed by anything?

"I like Mister Champion's notion about an open door," continued Rich. "Me and him think a lot alike. The only difference is that I know what I'm talking about and he doesn't."

He snapped that off, hurling the words out. "I learned the hard way," he said. "Champion got his notions about what this country is like out of a book. I got my ideas out of the faces and the hearts of the people who came here first. I wish Champion could have talked to my dad, General. My dad, he tried to take a hoe and a Georgia stock plow and make something in the plains. He didn't have a snowball's chance in hell. This country ain't like that back East where Mister Champion comes from. The northers come in the winter and the suns are hot in the summer. They eat crops up. The squatters die by droves and their life is just plumb hell on earth. I know, General. I was raised in a squatter's hut. I buried my dad with my own hands—what was left of him.

"I don't claim, General, that men like me oughta own this country. I don't deny that Mister Champion and his kind are gonna go along and some day there'll be an empire here like he dreams about. But that day ain't here now, General. Mister Champion talks about that open door. It wasn't open when *I* came here, General. It wasn't open anywhere in the West. It was locked and it was barred. But some Texas cattle outfits kicked it down and drove their herds through and we've been holding it open ever since. We figgered, like Mister Champion says, that we had the right to push on, that a man has the right to move ahead and then fight to hold what he has."

He looked around him and there was now a half grin on his lips. "Mister Pettigrew there, the lawyer from Kansas City, he talks about a notary and the way a paper is made out. Shucks, General, we ain't got notaries in this country. A man says he'll send me three thousand head of cattle and I tell him I'll take 'em. His word is *bueno* and so is mine. If we had to wait for lawyers, General, there never would be anybody moving through that open door Mister Champion talks about."

Rich stopped to let his eyes sweep the circle of faces. I had seen that half grin on his face before, when he was forking an outlaw, when he was spurring through the brush after a dogie.

He turned back to General Sheridan and he slowly took a paper out of his pocket.

"Here is my lease with the Arapahos," he said calmly. The grin had left his face. His was a hard look. "I sent all the way to Kansas," he added, "for a notary public to fix it up so Mister Pettigrew there could sabbe it. This notary, he talked to all of Catamo's tribe and got 'em to show they're stringing along with their chief by making their marks. This notary had a powwow with Catamo, General. It's all here just like Catamo said it. Catamo ain't hankering for any more deals with this Bob Purdy or with Walter

Jenson. Catamo says that of the money paid to Jenson the Indians got only tough beef. Jenson issued 'em culls and charged 'em like it was prime grass-fed stuff. All that is in writing, General, in case you want to use it."

Sheridan's face had not relaxed for a moment, nor his eyes left Rich's.

"Are you making a complaint?" he demanded.

"The Indians are," Rich shrugged. "Me, I ain't kicking, General. I'm not asking a thing except to be left alone to carry out my deal."

Sheridan took the document, bent his black head over it a moment in earnest study, then passed the lease on to Pettigrew.

"Now, General," Rich said, "I'd like to get moving. There are three thousand cattle out there in the flats, hungry and thirsty. If my lease is *bueno*, I'd like to get 'em moving."

It took the General a long moment to decide what to say. Most of that time he simply stared at Rich Stewart. There was nothing in his face to show what he was thinking.

Suddenly he bobbed his head. "Your lease is in order, Mr. Stewart," he said crisply. "The military is not disposed to interfere with you in any way."

There was a chorus of "yipees" from the riders who had been listening through the windows. There was a rush for their horses and then the clatter of hoofs as they raced for the trail herd without waiting for orders from their ramrod.

Maybe they didn't understand exactly what Sheridan said but they knew its import. A shrill-voiced yell floated back:

"Git along, little dogies!"

Back in the store the Kansas lawyer and this Martin Champion were remonstrating with the General. He listened a moment, then made a clicking sound with his teeth.

"Gentlemen, Washington is the only appeal."

He stomped out of the store without a backward look and on toward the hotel.

Rich grinned at me. "I'll bet you thought for a moment that they had my hide nailed to their fence."

"I sure did, pardner," I admitted. "But you put up a fair spiel yourself when you got wound up."

Patricia held out her hand. Rich held it a moment in both of his, then dropped it like it was a hot potato.

"I'm happy for you, Rich," she said. "And I'm proud of you. You certainly stood up to the bunch of them."

A happy gleam came into his eyes. "They got the jump on me with their highfalutin talk," he conceded, "but I'm picking up sabbe. I ain't quite as dumb as I used to be, Pat."

Then his face quickly hardened and Pat and I turned and there were Tim and Jeb Mulloy. They passed within an arm's reach of us but didn't give us a look.

"What are they up here for?" Pat whispered.

"Trailing Dad," I answered miserably.

"Then he's . . . !"

Rich interrupted. "Here is no place to gab about that," he said quickly. "Seems like your dad shook 'em and they're figgering he'll drift up this way. I'll handle that."

"No, Rich," Pat said firmly. "Not your way. Dad wouldn't want that."

"Sometimes," he protested, "my way is . . ."

"We'll talk about it at the hotel," Pat broke in. "Come along."

I started after them but Pat motioned me back. "No, Pete. Rich and I will settle this between the two of us."

"Reckon I can deal myself in if . . ." I demurred.

There was a quick gleam in her eyes. "No, Pete," she insisted. "Rich has you eating out of his hand."

She turned and almost collided with Martin Champion.

"My apologies, Madam," he said quickly, bowing slightly. "I only want to extend to Mr. Stewart my congratulations."

I couldn't blame Rich for grinning slightly. This Champion had struck me as being an even better speaker than the Kansas City lawyer; congratulations from him meant something.

"I'm afraid, Mr. Stewart," Champion said smoothly, "I have misjudged you. I thought all we would have to do would be to get you before a hearing and General Sheridan would cancel your lease immediately. But you beat us at our own game. You outtalked us."

His voice was pleasant and sincere but there was still a challenge in his tone and manner. Rich only bobbed his head; it was Pat who spoke, Pat with her hand lightly on Stewart's elbow.

"That's nice of you, Mr.—."

"Champion, Madam, Martin Champion," he replied with another bow.

"I am Miss Haines, Patricia Haines," Pat answered with poise and assurance. "This is my brother, Pete. We are . . ."

Champion's eyes gleamed. "You are the famous sweetheart from Texas," he murmured. "Mr. Stewart has sung your praises all over the territory, Miss Haines." He turned upon Rich. "And, Mr. Stewart," he said gallantly, "this is still another instance in which you are not, as you cowmen say, running a windy."

"Thank you," Pat answered, a red spot showing in each cheek.

She and Rich walked slowly toward the hotel. Martin Champion looked after them a moment. Then the Kansas lawyer joined him and I heard the attorney say:

"We'll never get anywhere with Sheridan, Martin. Won't your father help us?"

"Not with the present administration," Champion answered. "Should Cleveland get elected . . . well . . ."

They were walking off and I didn't hear any more.

Pat and Rich were still talking when I got to the hotel. Rich looked up with a rueful grin. "Your sister has laid the law down to me, pardner," he shrugged. "I can't sit in on the little game between your dad and the Mulloys unless I'm challenged."

"In five minutes," I reminded Pat, "Rich could scatter them Mulloys."

"Yes," Pat conceded. "He could."

She stood up.

"I have your promise, Rich?" she asked quietly.

He nodded. He made a helpless motion of his hands to me.

# CHAPTER FIVE

Things were humming in Cimarron. Rich and a handful of his men had already thrown up the frame building that was the home office of the Cimarron Cattle Company and they were enlarging the corrals to hold three thousand cattle.

All of the paper work had been tossed carelessly into my lap. I was to handle all of the pay rolls and to pay for the cattle coming up from Texas. I was to purchase supplies for the widely scattered Stewart riders and also to contract for what labor Rich and his boys didn't intend to do themselves. The first "minor chore" was to purchase fifty miles of barbed wire and contract for its delivery to the main camp in the Arapaho country.

"What about money?" I asked Rich. "All of this calls for plenty of cash."

"Lula Belle is the banker," he shrugged. "She has a safe in her place that nobody can break into. Write out an order. Lula Belle will honor it."

He must have noticed my look for he added: "You'll see the day, pardner," he said a little harshly, "that you'll claim Lula Belle is the finest lady in the Cimarron."

He was impatient to get away to the Arapaho

country camp and I didn't blame him; he wasn't the type of man who could be satisfied standing around while men built corrals. "Lemme ramrod this fence," I finally suggested, and he jumped at it. He was gone within an hour with nothing but a quick good-bye to Pat.

I observed that the four men Rich had hired in Lula Belle's saloon were driving two nails to a cowhand's one and sawing boards straight instead of every which way. I was sympathetic with the four line riders left here to finish this ignominious task. I hired three other drifters whose gnarled palms showed they were used to working with their hands and sent the line riders on to Rich.

These new men would work as long as I stood watching 'em; the minute my back was turned they laid down. They insisted on being paid at the end of every working day and they spent that day's wages at Lula Belle's every night. But they could handle lumber when they wanted to. Or when I made 'em. Husky, grinning Irishmen, they sweated by the gallon. I had to watch 'em every minute not only to keep 'em working but to see they didn't nail boards on any old way.

The corral was half-complete when one of the Scots approached me. They had camped behind the hotel, their wagons drawn up in a square like they were still on the prairie, and the men had spent most of their time loafing in front of

Champion's newspaper office, which was just across the dusty street from our building. Tim Mulloy was often in the middle of them, and sometimes buying drinks for them at the saloon. It was obvious the nesters had no intentions of leaving, and that Mulloy was mixing with 'em. I would have wondered more about that if I hadn't been so danged busy. It wasn't like cattlemen to drink with nesters.

This Scot introduced himself as Dennis Cameron. Several of his men, he said, wanted work.

I didn't like his sullen defiant manner but I needed men. We settled on a price, and I got a small pettish delight out of paying the Scots 25 cents a day less than I paid the Irishmen.

The Scots were better workers, too. The corral was finished the day before a dusty rider came into Cimarron asking for instructions. He had two thousand Texas shorthorns bedded down five miles from town.

Rich had told me cattle were coming but had left no instructions about brands or numbers. I asked for the purchase order. The Texan's face hardened.

"Don't reckon Rich can write any more than I can," he drawled. "There ain't any."

I had already bitten my tongue in regret at asking such a thing. Of course Rich didn't write out orders.

"Matter of fact," added the cattleman, "I never talked to Rich myself. Hy Moran just dropped off at my place and said Rich would take as many as I could bring up."

"Bring them in," I said.

The cattle were driven into the corral only after a hectic day which saw everybody in Cimarron almost driven wild by the swirling dust and by the shouting and stomping.

"How many?" I asked the Texan. He was Ray Magruder from the Palo Pinto country.

"Are you asking me," countered Magruder, "or are you figgering with me?"

I grinned. I had learned my lesson.

"I'm asking you," I said.

He shuffled his feet a moment while he chewed thoughtfully on his thin-cut.

"Started with right at two thousand head," he mused. "We lost eight swimming the Red. Then we let the Comanches cut out twelve head. Reckon about six or eight of 'em are on their last legs. We'll figger nineteen hundred and eighty, sonny."

"That's *bueno* with me," I said quickly.

"Come on," he said as I handed him his order, "I'll buy a drink."

I had to accept. And, I knew, to buy one around for Rich Stewart. This was the Wide S outfit and its gear was in good order and its riders a smart-looking lot. Lula Belle greeted Magruder by name. I was beginning to wonder how she knew every cattleman by sight. I learned later that she could tell the owner by the way he walked into the saloon and that she made it her business to find out who owned a herd, and who was straw bossing it, before the first hand came into town.

We were standing against the bar, Magruder and I, when Tim Mulloy and his cousin entered. Magruder quickly called out a greeting. The two men shook hands. Magruder motioned to the bar but Tim shook his head and stalked on.

"Never knew Mulloy was such an unsociable cuss," Magruder mumbled.

"It's me," I explained. "We came from the same part of Texas. Mulloy hates my family like poison."

"Your dad was Frank Haines?" Magruder said.

"Yes," I answered defiantly.

"Somebody claimed they saw him in Fort Worth," the Palo Pinto man said slowly.

I wasn't surprised that he seemed to know something about the flare-up in the Frio country. Gossip swept across this cattle region faster than it seemed humanly possible.

"What was he doing?" I asked hopefully.

"The fellow who told me," Magruder answered carefully, "didn't say."

I gathered by his attitude what he thought.

I bought a round for Rich and then excused myself. It was already dark and I was dog-tired.

Patricia had eaten supper but she sat at the table with me while I ate. I told her about buying the two thousand head of cattle.

"I wondered where you had been all day," she said crossly. "You didn't even come to the hotel for dinner."

It was the first time I had thought about it. Gosh, I hadn't stopped to eat all day.

"Been busy," I said carelessly.

"Yes, busy," she said. She looked away. "You're happy, Pete," she murmured. "You and Rich hit it off well together. I'm glad."

"You and him seem to get along, too," I grunted.

"I don't know," she murmured. "Sometimes I think we do. But Rich . . . he's so . . . so . . ."

"He'll do to ride the river with," I said quickly.

"Of course," she agreed. "I didn't mean anything like that. But, Pete, where is this leading? A cattle deal, a grass lease. It isn't a home. It isn't building anything."

"He stands to clean up a hundred thousand," I pointed out.

Then I remembered to tell her what Magruder had said about hearing of Dad.

"I've had the funniest feeling all day," she said. "I've felt like Dad was right close to us."

She sighed. "This shooting! This killing. I think about Rich, Pete. He has killed men. He'll kill more. Did he tell you anything about the Indians?"

"Believe he did say they had a run in every now and then," I said cautiously.

"I suppose no one will ever change him," she mused. "Danger is his life. I believe he actually loves it."

"Aw, quit the worrying," I said. "Dad is all right, and Rich is all right. Let's play a game of seven-up."

I was really too tired to enjoy playing but I could sense how lonely she was. We went out to the lobby and took over the round table and the greasy frayed deck of cards. Martin Champion sat there reading a newspaper from the East. He nodded. Patricia, I noticed, returned his greeting.

I lost the game and begged out of playing any more.

"I'm so tired I could sleep for a week," I explained.

As I stood up Martin Champion left his chair.

"Pardon me," he said in that polite way of his, "but I'd like to ask a few questions about the trail herd."

"What about 'em?" I demanded.

"I'd like information for my newspaper," he said. "How many head? Where from? And what price was paid?"

I glared at him. Patricia spoke up.

"Newspaper men usually want information like that for their paper, Pete," she explained.

"We bought a million head," I grinned. "They

came from China. We paid a million pesos in Mex money per head. The lead steer was named Baldy. He's smarter than some men I know. He doesn't ask questions about things that are none of his business."

"Pete," my sister snapped reprovingly.

With a chuckle at Martin Champion's reddening features I went on upstairs. I stopped and looked back. Champion accepted her apologies for my rudeness with a bow.

"I noticed you playing seven-up," he smiled showing his even white teeth. "I haven't played since I was a child. Would you consider playing a game with me?"

Patricia hesitated and I saw her eyes dart in my direction. I shook my head. But her eyes only flashed and her chin went up and she said:

"I'd be glad to."

I went on to my room with a helpless feeling. Some of Rich's business, I growled to myself, I just couldn't run for him.

Two days passed and no word from Rich. The cattle lapped up water and on the third day I had to scour the country around and buy feed for them. I sent a rider to the Cimarron camp and he returned with Rich's instructions to send 'em on.

Send 'em on! Who by!

I went to the saloon to ask Lula Belle's advice. I had to go and see her often these days. It took the two of us to piece together the loose ends of Rich Stewart's cattle deal. But I never took money from her without some qualms about it. I just didn't like having her kind of a woman for a partner.

"Rich said to leave things like that to you," she shrugged when I told her we had to have more riders. "Do you need money?"

"I reckon so," I nodded. Actually I had never asked her outright for any; I had just sort of hinted around.

Arch Witherspoon, the wrinkled old man Rich had left to handle the corral stock, had cattle sabbe. He said we could get along with four men. There were plenty of idle men in this strange territory town but I had to rustle some to find two half-breeds and two hoemen who would work for a cow outfit.

Arch came back in two days driving twenty of the same steers with him.

"Rich said to keep 'em," he explained. "Having some trail-broken leaders will make the next herd easier to handle."

I nodded. Arch or I should have thought of that.

Then I realized that if we kept a handful of steers in the corral we had to feed 'em. I started out trying to find some kind of hay. I propositioned Dennis Cameron but none of the Scots wanted to work for us.

"We work no more for Rich Stewart," Cameron said gruffly.

I looked around contemptuously. The Scots were living out of their wagons, cooking and sleeping on the ground.

"You think you can live this way all winter?" I demanded. "We can use a few men. And they can throw 'em up shacks behind the corral in their spare time. We'll furnish the lumber."

"No," he said firmly.

I wanted to turn on my heels with a sneer for him and his kind but I needed help so badly I stayed to argue.

"You want your wives and kids to starve to death?" I demanded.

"They won't starve, Pete," a voice said behind me.

Martin Champion was standing there.

"Mr. Cameron and these other men came out here with me," Champion stated calmly. "They are settlers accepted by the Cimarron Land and Colonization Company. I promised them land and I'm responsible for them until they get it."

I stared at him, wondering if he was as well-heeled as he hinted or if he was trying to run a windy.

"There's some business we can do with you," he went on. "These people need meat. We'll pay delivery prices."

"We'd shoot our steers," I snapped, "before we would let a nester eat 'em."

"As you wish," Champion shrugged.

I turned back to the saloon. Lula Belle, I thought miserably, would have to handle this. I couldn't hire any hay cutters.

Tim Mulloy and his cousin were standing in front of the saloon. Tim was rolling a smoke. He gave me a sharp look.

"Here's the button," Jeb sneered. "Wish his pop had the guts to show up."

"None of that, Jeb," Tim said quickly. To me he added: "Sorry, youngster. Jeb ain't ever learned not to shoot off his mouth."

"There ain't any Haines afraid of either of you," I sung out. "And, Jeb, if you're so danged nervy, why haven't you looked up Rich Stewart?"

Tim's hand fell on my shoulder. I thrust it off. "Let it lay, youngster," he advised me in a voice that was gruff but not unkind. "Jeb here don't count. Frank Haines and me can settle what's between us on our own. I just got Jeb along for the company."

"Danged poor company," I snapped.

"I didn't get to pick my relatives," Tim said.

I stared at Tim. Somehow it seemed unreal to me that this thin-faced man was actually hounding my father, intending to kill him on sight. I remembered Skip, and Skip had looked just like his dad.

"My dad isn't coming up here," I told Tim. "What are you hanging around for?"

Tim went back to making his smoke. He finished it and stuck it in the corner of his mouth before answering. Then he said, low and flat: "I thought as much of my kid as Frank Haines did of you. I'm sticking around, youngster."

He lit the cigarette. Then, with a droop to his lips: "I ain't wasting my time, youngster. You can tell your compadre that I'm figgering on going in the cattle business up here."

My face must have showed my shock for he shrugged his lean shoulders and added: "Natural thing, ain't it? I figger on being here a spell. Might as well pick up some chips while I'm about it."

He waited a moment, then added with a thin smile: "You can tell your compadre that."

I nodded and went on. Lula Belle listened to my tale of woe and agreed to send over to the next town for some help. And also to put her two Indian handy men out to cutting and curing grass.

I mentioned what Mulloy had said. She nodded. She seemed to know everything that went on.

"Mulloy is aiming to start a spread," she explained. "He has sent for some riders."

"Where?"

Her troubled eyes met mine. "I'd guess in the Arapaho country," she said.

"In Rich's country!"

"Yes."

"Then, by Gum," I declared, "he'll get more trouble than he's looking for. I wish he would cross Rich. Then Rich would settle our feud along with his."

"Your dad," she said softly, "was in the Kiowa settlement last week. Looks like he's heading this way."

I studied her face trying to figure out whether or not she knew any more about him.

"If he shows up," she volunteered, "I'll slip out to Rich's camp."

I thanked her and started back to the hotel. A small crowd was gathered in front of Champion's office and Martin himself stood with a stack of papers.

"It's off," he called to somebody behind me. "First copies of the Cimarron *Bugle*. No charge for the first copy."

He handed me a paper before he saw who I was. His cheeks were ruddier than ever and he could hardly talk for his excitement.

"Oh, hello, Pete," he said with a quick change of tone. I noticed how he stiffened as I looked at the still-damp newspaper.

The first thing I saw was the black type over his front-page editorial:

HOMESTEADERS MUST NOT GIVE UP
The Fight Between Rich Stewart and the
Home Builder Must Not Be Abandoned

I read on. Champion had written:

> Rich Stewart has sent his first herd of wild longhorns storming into rich Arapaho country. The first victory belongs to this ruthless Texan who has no concern for the plight of the home-seeking pioneers pouring into the Cimarron.
> But the fight is not over. It has not yet begun. Settlers are pouring into Cimarron. They want to build homes.
> They want to clear land and push their plows into this rich virgin soil. This is the march of empire, and neither Rich Stewart nor any other man can stay it.
> The sturdy pioneers who have followed the westward stars to the Cimarron will not turn back because of Rich Stewart.

I looked up from the paper. The Scots were watching me, standing off a little, their faces grim. Martin Champion was regarding me with tight lips.

I wadded up the paper and jammed it into my pocket. "You're asking for trouble," I said hotly.

"I know," Martin answered quietly. "But I think we're right, Pete."

I glared around at the Scots. I had a cattleman's feeling for them, a sense of superiority. But I wasn't denying their backbone. Nesters, I knew full well, were the most stubborn breed of men molded by the Almighty; I had seen enough of them in Texas to know that. But I had seen something else in Texas, too—the impressive grim determination with which a cowman fought for his grass.

"You're nothing but a damned fool," I told Champion scornfully. "Why don't you go back East where you belong?"

I thought he would jump me for that. I had never seen a man take talk like that—on his feet. He did turn red. But he just kept looking at me without saying a word in reply. With a short laugh I swaggered by him, pushing him a little with my shoulder. From now on, now that they had tipped their hand, these nesters would have to take that from me and my kind.

I walked on to the corral.

"Arch," I said to the wrinkle-faced old timer, "ride out and tell Rich to bring a few boys in with him. I'll watch the corral."

It was about eight o'clock when Rich galloped in with four boys.

"What's up?" he demanded.

I read him what Champion had written about him. I told him about Dennis Cameron's refusal to work for us and Tim Mulloy's hint that he was gonna start a spread up here.

"Thought Tim might deal himself in," he said.

He sighed. "We'll get a drink. Then we'll eat.

Tell Luke at the hotel to fix up five meals. We'll be right down."

I hadn't eaten myself so I told Luke to make it six. The dining room was closed and the cook gone; the hotel man had to do the cooking himself.

In the lobby were Patricia and Martin Champion. She was holding two books in her lap.

"Mr. Champion," she explained, "was nice enough to lend me something to read."

I called her off to one side, with no apology to the newspaper man.

"Rich is at the saloon," I said. "He's coming here to eat in a minute. I wouldn't let him see me with Champion if I were you."

"Why not?"

"Did you see what his newspaper printed about Rich?"

"Yes." Her lips tightened. "Mr. Champion doesn't see things like we do. That's because he was raised different."

"Whose girl are you?" I demanded. "You know you got to take Rich's side."

"I'm not a cowhand to be bossed around by a sixteen-year-old straw boss," she snapped. "The authority Rich is giving you is making a plumb fool out of you, Pete."

With that she whirled around. She didn't go back to sit by Champion, but hurried on upstairs.

Champion still sat where he was, looking after

her. I grunted to myself. It would serve him right if Rich came in and found him. But I felt a little sorry for him. The poor fool didn't know what might happen.

"Look, friend," I said coldly, "Rich Stewart is down at the saloon. He's coming here pronto. If you're smart, you'll think of business you have somewhere else."

His eyebrows formed a V. He thought over what I had said. Then I realized that this Champion did have a notion of what might pop.

"I've paid for my room," he said calmly. "I understood that my room rent included the privilege of sitting in the lobby and reading a paper or a book, or just sitting. Thanks, anyhow, Pete."

I turned away with a sigh.

Then Rich came into the hotel, his four riders at his heels. He stopped when he saw Champion. His shoulders dropped to a point, his weight hung forward on his toes as he came on slowly. Champion continued reading. Stewart looked down at him a moment, then went on into the dining room.

I joined them and we put away a fair-sized hunk of steak each and a double cut of apple pie. Rich ordered a second cup of coffee and drank it slowly while he smoked a cigarette and we talked of casual matters, how the Magruder herd had been in tiptop shape and how the lightning storms might break into rain any day now. Champion read his book in plain sight of Rich. Not once, however, did Rich look in the newspaper man's direction.

Then Rich pushed back his chair.

"Come on, boys," he said grimly, "we got work to do."

I followed them outside. There were crowbars and axes piled up on the front porch. Rich took one of each. His four hands followed suit.

"Stay out of this, Pete," Rich told me. "You're the business manager."

I watched from the walk in front of the hotel. They battered down the door to Martin Champion's newspaper office. With crowbars and axes they began to demolish his equipment.

He stepped outside, Champion did.

"See what happens to guys who get too big for their britches," I jeered.

His face was florid and grim. "You can tell your hard-riding friend," he snapped, "that this isn't the end. It's just the beginning."

With that he turned and stalked back into the hotel.

A crowd gathered. There were the Scots, quiet, impassive, hanging back on the edges. There was Tim Mulloy, lean, unsmiling, aloof. There were girls from Lula Belle's squealing in excitement and cheering as Rich rolled Champion's printing press out into the street and smashed it again and again with a crowbar. There was Lula Belle herself, in a velvet gown this time, her flesh gleaming white in the dark.

Type was scattered all over the dust of the street. A jar of ink was smashed and formed a black pool in the dirt; a roll of paper was unwound and torn into shreds.

They worked an hour. Then Rich yelled for all to join 'em at Lula Belle's for a drink on him.

"And then one on the house," Lula Belle's voice sang out. "Come on, boys and gals. We'll drink to Rich Stewart and the Cimarron Cattle Company!"

With yells and squeals some of the spectators trooped after them. Rich put his arm around Lula Belle and they walked into the saloon that way.

I heard a choking sob behind me. Patricia was standing there.

She seemed to notice me for the first time. "I suppose," she said in a strange voice, "this thrills you."

"No more than it does Rich," I answered. "It was something that had to be done. He did it."

The Scots were going back to their camp. Then the only man left standing before the wreckage was Tim Mulloy. I wondered what he was thinking. Then I shivered and turned back to the hotel. I didn't want to know.

# CHAPTER SIX

In the morning Champion came down to breakfast while Pat, Rich and I were finishing up. He gave us a curt nod, then took a table a few feet from us.

His appearance put the quietus on our flow of talk. I regretted that; it was the first time since we had come to Cimarron that we had gabbed in our old way. Rich had seemed in anything but a hurry and he had been teasing Patricia, and buttering her up some too. She needed a lot of both. She hadn't been noticed nearly enough, not by the right man anyhow, since we had checked in at Luke's hotel.

We finished and Rich stopped by Champion's table as we went out.

"Understand there was something of a ruckus last night," he said.

"So I understand," was the quick, cold reply. "I haven't been down to check up yet on the damage."

"Seems to have been considerable," Rich murmured. "That's one of the bad things about living in a cow country town, Champion. Boys gotta cut loose their wolf every now and then. Figger up the damage and send me the bill."

Champion shook his head. "As you say,

Stewart," he answered carefully, "that goes with settling in this type of country. Whatever the damage is, I'll figure it as a part of the overhead."

That wasn't the kind of reply Rich had expected, not at all. I saw the corners of his mouth quirk as if he were tempted to smile. But he only nodded.

We stepped out of the hotel. Off in the distance there was a cloud of dust as some rider headed toward Cimarron on the double quick.

"I imagine," Rich sighed, "that's one of my boys."

It was. The dusty sweating man rolled out of his saddle and shuffled toward us as fast as his high heels would let him.

"Come quick, Rich," he panted. "Limpy got his."

"How?" demanded Stewart.

"Indians," was the terse answer. "Arapahos."

Rich turned back to the hotel.

"Can I go along?" I asked eagerly. I had never seen the main camp. Besides, I was getting fed up with office work and administrative details.

"*Bueno*," Rich agreed.

The three of us made tracks. I would have preferred a slower pace, for this was new country to me. I liked it. The new grass was beginning to show in the brown plains, drawn up by a sun whose heat was tempered by cool breezes touched with the lush damp smell of fair rains.

Yes, cattle would fatten here, I thought happily. A longhorn would put on forty pounds in a single feeding season. And every pound was money in the bank.

Near night we received our first challenge—we had not ridden a direct route but had cut deeper into the hills to study and to confirm the story that a war party of Arapahos had dipped into Rich's country. We were hailed by a lone man who was careful to recognize Rich before showing us a light by which to dismount.

He took our horses and led them off; I pushed after Rich into the one-room sod house which served as a bunkhouse for all of his crew. It was what I had expected—mattresses of buffalo grass, blankets which hadn't been washed in many a day. A gnarled mustached man was laboring over a sheet-iron stove; he wiped flour from his palms and shook hands with me. He was Pecos Sherrill, the cook.

"Chow's nearly ready," Pecos said curtly.

Rich sat down and rolled a cigarette. I could sense how eager he was to learn what had happened. It was maddening the way Pecos picked up the steaks, tossed them into the boiling fat, wiped the flour from his hands again, and only then was willing to talk to his boss.

"I sent Stoney for you," Sherrill said. "The boys are fit to be tied."

"It was Limpy?" asked Rich. I had to admire

the way he could control his impatience. But, knowing cowhands, I realized there was no point of trying to rush Pecos into telling his story. It would come out in Sherrill's own good time.

"Yep. Arapahos."

"Where?"

"The south fence." Pecos talked in a casual dull undertone.

"Limpy riding alone?"

Sherrill nodded, then added: "Shot down from the bush, Rich. Not a chance to fight back."

"Where is everybody?" Rich asked.

I had wanted to ask the same question. This was the headquarters camp but we had seen only two men.

"Burying Limpy," Pecos said tersely, turning back to his steaks.

Rich continued to smoke. I looked around the dugout, fascinated by all the gear piled up here. There were saddles and boxes of cartridges and a roll of rope and two coils of barbed wire. The smell of soiled clothing and tobacco hung heavy, too heavy. There were tobacco sacks everywhere and crumpled papers and discarded clothing. This place, I thought, could stand a good cleaning.

Now we could hear the men outside tromping around. They came through the dugout door and I saw a group of men who greeted their employer with curt nods and pulled up chairs and sat in grim tense silence. None of them sat in his chair right, either tilting it way back or sitting in it backwards, resting their heads and shoulders on the backs. Rich smoked another cigarette. He wasn't looking at his men but at the sputtering steaks.

"Limpy," he said slowly, breaking the strained silence, "was a good man to ride with. I first ran into him in Ellsworth."

"Yeah," one of the dark scowling men remembered. "He was sweet on a gal up there."

Rich threw down his cigarette. "I hate to lose a man," he murmured. "Any man. And Limpy was a good one. Those looked like Arapaho tracks to me. But I ain't sure. The Arapahos signed a treaty with me. Some white men never give an Injun credit for sticking to his word. I do."

He looked around him challengingly.

"I'll ride up to see the big chiefs tomorrow and find out what the deal is," he proposed.

One of the riders had a scar on his right cheek which was blazing an unholy purple.

"Reckon, Rich," he said grimly, "we'd better pay the Arapahos a visit on our own. They did it. I can tell an Arapaho's tracks from a Cherokee's. I think if we rough up one of their villages, they'll get the idea and leave us alone."

"If you do that, Black John," Stewart answered slowly, "you gotta draw your time first. I can't have trouble between my men and the Arapahos. When Yankee troops come in, out I go."

Black John's answer was to jerk his thumb toward the west, I suppose in the direction of Limpy's grave.

"I know," Rich sighed. He twisted his hands and scowled at the stove. "I don't like it either, boys," he added. "But you knew how the hand had to be played when you came up here. You'll have to string along with me."

"That's hard to do, Rich," spoke up Pecos from the stove.

His tone was mild, but there was nothing timid about it.

"I know it," Stewart nodded.

He didn't say anything else. He just sat and smoked. Pecos put the steaks on the table and not a man made a motion in that direction. Rich wasn't looking at them, but at the packed dirt floor. And they looked everywhere but at him.

"Them steaks," Pecos said finally, "ain't gonna stay hot forever."

Black John was the first man to move his chair closer to the table. The others followed suit. Rich was the last. Except for the gleam in his eyes, his expression hadn't changed since he had entered the bunkhouse.

There was no formal agreement but it was easy to see that, without having an argument about it, Rich Stewart had won his point. And why shouldn't he, I thought loyally? They were riding men of the same breed as I was.

Rich and I rode toward the Arapaho main camp the next morning. As we loped along, he explained the lay of the country to me and pointed out landmarks along the way. The Chisholm trail, he said, was to the east and for a long time Texans did not venture into the Arapaho country.

"I was ramrodding Chet Miller's spread," he recalled, "and we ran into some guerillas who laid down an ambush for us. We fought 'em off but they picked up men and laid in wait for us. I made a deal with Catamo, the head man of the Arapahos. For fifty cows, he not only let us pass through his country but sent out a war party to scare the guerillas off. Me and Catamo have been pardners ever since. The Arapahos are pretty good Indians. Smart, too. They size up a herd coming through and make their play in the open."

I remembered hearing other Texans cuss at having to cut out beef for the Arapahos.

"That's only fair," shrugged Rich when I brought that up. "The Indian is kicked around plenty. We take his best grass and drive his buffalo off. I like to get along with 'em. But sometimes you can't.

"The trouble," he added, "is that Indians make the same mistake we do. We figger all red men are alike. They figger all white men are alike. Some red men never could get along with some white men. But then some white men can't get along either."

I thought about the Mulloys and the Haines. "I reckon," I agreed, "we can show 'em a thing or two about holding a hate."

He knew what I was thinking about.

"Heard anything about your dad lately?" he asked after a moment.

"Nothing else."

"I picked up a little news," he said thoughtfully and with seeming reluctance. "Frank didn't run from Tim Mulloy, but from the law. They called it murder. Mulloy posted a reward. They know that your dad got over the Red and into the Territory."

I stared at Rich. Did he know more than he was telling me?

"Had quite a ruckus down there," he went on in the same unwilling manner. "Mulloy was in the posse that came after your dad. They thought they had him, they raided the house after dark and he was in it. But he got out somehow. They think they winged him. But he shook 'em off his trail. He got to Doan's."

He took a deep puff on his cigarette, then threw it away.

"Wouldn't be surprised," he murmured, "if Frank turns up any time now."

"Rich, have you heard from him?" I demanded.

"Of him," he shrugged. His eyes twinkled at me. "I wouldn't hold out on you, pardner," he promised. "The day Frank Haines gets in touch with me, I'll let you know."

I wondered what would happen if my dad just rode into Cimarron in the wide-open daylight. All sorts of ideas popped into my head. Maybe Rich could . . .

We reached the Indian camp just before noon. Their kettles were a-steaming and the aromas made my innards quiver in anticipation. We had eaten breakfast before daylight and had ridden at a steady pace all morning.

"Will they feed us?" I asked Rich anxiously.

"That's why I wanted to get here around noon," he answered. "If Catamo offers us grub, it's a sure sign he is still friends with us. If he is on the warpath, or thinks my boys are pushing his people too hard, he'll starve us out."

Which was, I reflected, just about what you could expect of any white man.

It was the first time I had ever ridden into an Indian camp and I guess my eyes popped out at the squaws, the papooses, the indifferent warriors, the lodges and the tepees. Their horses were hobbled at the edge of their camp and one of my notions about Indians was exploded; they were pretty sorry nags. I had always figured Indians tore over the prairie on the finest mounts.

Rich lifted his hand every now and then in a dignified salute to a warrior he recognized but he rode on to a big earth-roofed lodge before dismounting. A squaw was pounding corn in front of the lodge. She eyed us without missing a lick with her rocks.

"Isn't Catamo here?" I asked Rich after a moment in which no one had come forward to greet us.

"Sure," he grinned. "Catamo ain't in a hurry. He's a big chief. He'd keep anybody waiting."

Just as he spoke, Catamo emerged from the lodge. Again I was shocked; he wasn't my idea of what an Indian chief would be at all. He was old and his chest seemed to have shrunk in and the muscles in his long arms had withered up. He didn't look to me like he weighed over a hundred and twenty pounds, though he must have been at least six feet tall. His eyes flashed as he recognized Rich, and they seemed to be intelligent eyes. He looked curiously at me and then asked Rich something in his dialect.

Rich answered, then explained to me with a smile: "He wants to know if you are my son."

Catamo motioned for us to be seated and they chattered away in the Arapaho tongue. Remembering my feeble efforts to learn Latin in my two years of advanced schooling, I marveled at how easily Rich Stewart had mastered this Indian tongue which had been as foreign to him as Latin was to me. He not only understood the dialect, he talked it fluently.

I was busting to know what was being said

but Rich took his own sweet time telling me.

"He says there are bad men among the Arapahos like among the white men," Rich finally explained. "He says there is a young chieftain who was not consulted about the lease with me and his feelings are hurt. The young chief is named Icado and some of the Arapahos are foolish enough to believe in him. Icado claims some of the land belongs to his tribe and he intends to make a different lease, with another white man."

Right off I knew who.

"Tim Mulloy?"

Rich nodded. "He says Icado's people have plenty of fresh beef and they are sneering at Catamo and Motiqo for being friends with me. If it was an Arapaho who killed Limpy, it must be one of Icado's braves."

He turned to the chief again. They talked back and forth. There was a quirk to Rich's mouth as he interpreted to me.

"I asked him if he couldn't control Icado," he explained. "He said no more than I could make white men behave. Jenson, the Indian agent, is throwing his weight around."

I had been trying to make up for my inability to understand the tongue by studying every flicker of emotion on Catamo's face. The aged Indian seemed honestly regretful of Limpy's murder.

Catamo lifted his hand in a gesture to the squaw

still pounding away at her corn and Rich grinned at me.

"Now we eat," he said.

I sighed in anticipation. But, when I held the bowl full of strange looking stew in my hands, I couldn't work up too much of an appetite for it. It smelled all right, it even tasted fair. Maybe it was the color. Or maybe it was some secret premonition for, when riding back to camp, Rich told me carelessly that it was probably dog meat, I felt like vomiting up what little I had eaten.

We galloped along a while as if intending to reach the main camp by sundown. Then, in midafternoon, Rich suddenly pulled up his horse.

"We need a hunt," he said. "We need a side of venison in our camp. I got things to do but they can wait. It's been a long time since we hunted together, hasn't it?"

"Too blamed long," I answered quickly.

Rich pointed toward a wooded ridge. "With this sun," he pointed out, "the deer will be sleeping in there. I'll work around behind the ridge and run a buck right into your lap."

I crouched in a clump of bear grass where I could watch the wooded ridge from all sides. I knew it would be a long time; a hunter like Rich worked slowly. I watched the tops of the trees for telltale signs, particularly for blue jays. I heard one squawk and saw it soar straight up and I gripped my gun. There was a stirring ahead of me and I was ready when out of the brush leaped a lithe dun body topped by the shadows of horns. He gave me a set shot but I didn't want it. I waited 'til he got my scent, 'til he pawed the ground in uncertainty, then leaped at an angle back for the shelter of the timber.

I hit him in mid-air right under the shoulder. He leaped high, plumb over a clump of bushes. For a moment my heart was in my mouth. Had I just winged him? Would I have to face my pardner with the shamed admission that I had missed and that we would have to track down a wounded buck in the brush?

Another long leap, then the deer crumpled all at once. I ran up and was busy with my hunting knife when Rich came gliding through the timber, making no sound at all. That was always something that set Rich apart from the other cowhands. He could walk like an Indian or a mountain man, even in his boots.

It was a five-pointer and great eating. We roasted a thick steak each and darned if Rich didn't know how to season the meat with berries and wild herbs. We gorged ourselves. Then, as our fire burned low, we stretched out on our blankets and Rich smoked while lying flat on his back. It was the first time I ever wanted a cigarette. Rich had to finally roll it for me.

"This is the life, pardner," Rich murmured.

"Nothing to worry about, our bellies full. The sky above us is friendly and peaceful and the brush is kinda glad we're around."

I nodded and tossed another mesquite root on the fire. We didn't need the heat but I liked the warm comforting glow.

"Funny about a campfire," Rich said drowsily. "They always seems to soothe a man. I can remember a lot of 'em. Once, in Wyoming . . ."

His words fell off into a snore. He went right to sleep in the middle of a sentence.

I wasn't far behind him.

We were riding before sunup the next morning and Rich had all of his usual restless energy. He talked slow and usually walked with a deliberate tread, but the heart and the head underneath this leathery impassiveness worked like twin trip-hammers.

"I'll look up this Icado," he told me as we neared the camp. "And I'd better humor the boys along a few days. You get on back to Cimarron, pardner, and take care of things there."

I sighed. Back to the corral and the figures! Rich evidently sensed my reluctance to return to town for his fingers gripped my shoulder:

"Next year," he promised, "we'll be in the chips. Then we'll hire us a business manager and you can ride the same trail as me."

I nodded. Then I asked about Tim Mulloy's lease with Icado.

"Wouldn't Sheridan have to show Mulloy the same right as you?" I demanded.

He bobbed his head. His lips tightened. "Ever light a prairie fire?"

I shook my head. "I've been figgering about Mulloy," he murmured. "One way to fight a fire is to start a backfire."

"If Mulloy," I reasoned, "moves in on you, your boys will pop down on 'em. Mulloy's hands will fight back. Then Sheridan will stop the whole business."

"Could be," he shrugged. He sighed. "Then Tim may just see a chance to cut under me. I wouldn't hold that against him. He was raised that way. Grass belongs to the man who can get it, and keep it."

"We did you a dirty trick," I thought aloud, "when we came up here. If we hadn't come, Mulloy would have stayed in Texas."

"There was Purdy last year," he said. "There is Mulloy this year, maybe. There will be another one. It ain't ever a cinch, Pete.

"Speaking of your dad," he said after a moment, "keep a sharp eye out for signs of him. Get a rider out to me with whatever you hear of him."

I nodded and turned back toward the ugly little town of Cimarron.

# CHAPTER SEVEN

Within a week Champion had his paper going again. He rescued most of the type which had been scattered over the street and brought in a printer who restored the press. The printer spent most of his time, and all of his money, at Lula Belle's.

His second issue came off the press that Friday. He stopped me coming into the hotel and presented me with a copy.

"The format," he said dryly, "isn't as handsome. But I have ordered new type and another press. In a short time I can resume business as usual."

I studied the paper. There was nothing in it like his bombastic editorial in the first issue. In fact, I couldn't even find any mention of Rich's name.

"You're learning," I said. "Stay off Rich and you'll get along."

His eyes twinkled. "I haven't forgotten Mr. Stewart's little escapade," he said dryly. "But I think it won't be too long until the freedom of the press is guaranteed in Cimarron."

I wasn't sure what he was talking about.

"I rather think," he went on, "that by the end of the week Cimarron will be a law-abiding town."

He said no more. I shrugged my shoulders and went over to the corral. We had only fifty head of stock inside the fences but getting enough hay for them was a problem. The Scots doggedly refused to work for us.

It seemed to me that almost every day a new wagon rolled into Cimarron and a new brood of kids started their squealing play over the flats. And on Sunday morning a train of three wagons pulled up before Champion's office. Canvas tops concealed the contents of the wagons. Just about everybody turned out in curiosity.

The wagons belonged to a Jew named Nathan Stool. He had come from Arkansas to open a general store.

From Foley I got the details.

"Champion encouraged him," Foley said sourly. "I was Rich's man and I said so. Champion said that being the case, they'd bring another store man in here. Stool is their man."

That very afternoon a drove of the Scots started work on a store building for this Nathan Stool. He was a wiry little man with the small dark features of his race. He tried to work himself, but he smashed his thumb with a hammer and retired to a supervisory role.

In two days his store was up and he was ready for business. I walked back and forth in front of his place looking over his stock of goods. His building was rough and unpainted but it was big and the shelves and counters seemed to be groaning from the weight of implements, supplies and dress goods. He had hoes for sale, and Georgia stock plows, and harness. There were bolts of gingham and kegs of nails and cooking utensils. Stool, I thought, had come to this country well-heeled. He opened up for business with more on his shelves than Foley had ever had.

It was to be, I observed, a homesteader's store. Stool had some saddles and high-heeled boots but no self-respecting cowpoke would use 'em. They were mail-order stuff for dudes.

Rich rode in and showed little or no interest in the new store, nor in Champion's revival of the newspaper. He looked a little tired as we sat in Lula Belle's and heard what he had found out about Icado.

"He's a bad Indian," Rich said slowly. "He won't look me straight in the eye. And Mulloy is promising 'em more for a lease than I am paying Catamo."

"What can Icado do about it?"

"The Arapahos have been assigned the land," he explained. "Right now there is agitation for the southern half of their territory to be open for homesteading. That's where this Champion came in. My lease stops him even if he could get the land opened up. He passed the word around that he had an inside track in Washington and the Arapaho country would be split and the south part opened to homesteaders. Of course he ain't getting anywhere with it. My lease stops that."

"But Mulloy and Icado—what can they do to you?" I asked again. I knew all about Champion's peeve.

"They're Arapahos," he shrugged. "Part of the land is theirs. If they renounce my lease, they can sign with Mulloy. Then it's a question of which grass is mine and which his."

Lula Belle brought him a drink. "The only way out," he said, looking for her approval, "is to make a deal with Mulloy. Two outfits can't work the same range."

She nodded. "There's Tim now," he said.

The lean ranchman and his cousin stood at the bar with their backs to us.

Rich gnawed his lip. I could appreciate how this went against the grain. It wasn't like Rich to ever take a backward step.

He pushed back his chair, hitched at his belt and strolled over to Mulloy. The two turned and watched him with narrow eyes, neither speaking.

"Understand, Mulloy," Rich said, "you're interested in the Arapaho country?"

"Been looking at it," Tim nodded. "And ran into a fellow named Purdy the other day. He's got a lease but he is short on chips. I might make a deal with him, Stewart. Been thinking it over."

"I got the word," Rich murmured, "that the deal is already made."

"Could be," Mulloy shrugged.

Rich's tall frame heaved in a sigh. "There is enough grass up there for both of us," he said slowly, and painfully. "I had figgered on fifty thousand head of Texas cattle before spring. I won't make that."

"No," agreed Mulloy.

"This business of playing one Indian against another," continued Stewart, "it's bad. I'll make a deal, Mulloy. You and Purdy stay . . ."

Mulloy's voice broke in harsh, unyielding:

"Nobody asked you for a deal, Stewart."

Rick rocked back and forth on his high heels. "No," he admitted, "nobody did. But there is such a thing as killing the goose that lays the golden eggs."

"I'll take my chances," Mulloy shrugged.

Rich's shoulders dropped slightly. "Anything personal in this, Mulloy?" he asked softly.

Tim studied him a moment before answering. "No," he said carefully. "I thought there might be at first, Stewart," he added in frank explanation. "I want a man and I want him bad. You're that man's friend. You may be hiding him now for all I know. I got a hunch that you are. But this notion of mine to start a spread up here, it ain't personal."

"*Bueno*," murmured Stewart. "I'll take your word for it."

"I'm not passing up a bet like this, Stewart," Tim went on in his low flat voice. "You'll be out of here before spring."

A gleam of sardonic amusement showed in his eyes. "And without me doing one damned thing about it," he added.

Rich came back to the table. We sat in gloomy silence a moment. Lula Belle spoke first.

"Is Icado getting whiskey?" she asked.

Rich nodded.

Lula Belle reached over and took a gulp out of Rich's glass. "Tim's boys will hang around here some," she said. "I'll get the girls to work on 'em."

She went off to her roulette game. Rich looked after her with a faint smile.

"She's all wool and a yard wide, that gal," he murmured.

"She's a compadre of yours," I admitted. For some reason I had a jealous feeling about Lula Belle. Rich was supposed to marry my sister, not her.

"Look, pardner," I said awkwardly, "this ain't none of my business, I know. But I think the sooner you and Pat get hitched up, the better off for both of you."

I wasn't thinking about Lula Belle alone either. There was Martin Champion, polite and attentive to Patricia, lending her books to read, playing seven-up with her in the hotel lobby while I labored over my records and Rich was off in the Arapaho country riding herd on his steers.

"Pat had a notion," I pointed out, "that you'd get hitched right after she got here."

"I know," he nodded. His fingers drummed on the table. "I'm straining at the bit myself," he confessed. "But there's one thing holding me back. This spread I'm running, I promoted it. I didn't have but a couple of thousand myself. Until I nurse these cows through the winter and fatten 'em on Arapaho country grass, I ain't got a dime of my own."

"I see," I agreed.

"I'm not my own man yet," he said harshly. "Come spring, I'll be clear. Plenty clear."

"Spring," I observed, "is a long time off. Pat gets awful lonesome."

"It's hell on her," he conceded. "But I can't take time off for courting and getting married now. When you're sitting in a game short, friend, you can't throw in that hand and wait for a new deal. You gotta play the cards you got in that hand."

I could see that. He finished his drink and we went back to the hotel. He was off again the next morning.

Things were dull for a few days, except for another issue of Champion's newspaper. This came out on Tuesday, which he promised would be the regular publication date from now on.

The front-page story that citizens of Cimarron would meet in Nathan Stool's general store on Wednesday night to form a township brought a ripple of laughter from the customers at Lula Belle's.

"Seems to me," jeered one cowboy, "that this Champion is running for office."

I hadn't thought about going to the meeting but Pat asked me to accompany her. We were a little late; Champion was already addressing the Scots and the handful of other would-be homesteaders when we arrived.

"Friends, the building of a town is never easy," he warned. "At present there is no land available for homesteading except south of the river. But those of us who see the future of Cimarron want to start building *now.* Mr. Stool has already opened his store. Mr. Cameron's cousin has sent back East for the equipment with which to open another blacksmith's shop. I have received a letter from a friend of mine in Kentucky, a young physician, who is on his way to open his office. Cimarron will grow. Let those of us who believe in her future form our township *now.* In unity there is strength."

He was roundly applauded. Dennis Cameron, the dour Scot, spoke next.

"Aye, we need a town," he said in his gruff terse way. "We are here to stay. Many of us, we are going to file for land when Mr. Champion has it opened."

Nathan Stool spoke. "Ve haf a goot newspaper," he said, every word a struggle. "Ve haf a goot man in Mister Champion. Ve make him mayor of Cimarron! Vot!"

There was an answering roar. I suppose Patricia and I were the only ones who didn't join in the clamor.

Martin Champion smiled. "My friends," he announced, "I accept."

I nudged Pat. "Let's leave."

She agreed, but reluctantly.

Later on, I wished I had stayed to the end of the meeting. For then I would have been halfway prepared at least for the coming of Al Poggin.

Champion's door was open and he sat at his pine-topped desk writing letters.

"Hi, Mayor," I called in, yielding to a sudden notion. Most of the time I passed by him with no more than a nod.

"Come into the enemy's lair, Pete," he invited, pushing his writing away.

I hesitated a moment, then stepped inside and stood there ill at ease.

"I've been wanting to talk to you, Pete," he said slowly. "Sit down there."

"You might think it's none of my business," he went on, reaching for his curved-stemmed pipe and filling its blackened bowl from his pouch, "but I'd like to know the Haines' side of the story."

"What story?" I demanded.

"About your father—and Tim Mulloy."

"You print a danged word in your paper and . . ." I started to threaten.

"I'm not printing such things in my paper, Pete," he interrupted quickly. "I've heard Mulloy's side. I'd like to know yours."

I studied him suspiciously. "You and Mulloy are mighty thick," I growled.

He nodded. "In a business way. We are partners."

"Then to hell with you for still another reason," I snapped.

He wasn't offended by my answer. "We are partners," he went on. He puffed on his pipe a moment, studying me over its bowl. "Pete," he asked, "who is wrong in a grass war?"

"What do you mean?"

"You have 'em in Texas. There is open land. One outfit gets in first. The other outfit has to have it to keep going. They start feuding over it. Which is wrong?"

"The second outfit," I said promptly.

He smiled. "Let's put it another way. Let's get down to cases. I came from the East. Up there I heard about country that might be opened up soon, the Arapaho country. I launched a colonization company and filed a claim for land to build a town on. I get down here and I find another outfit on the spot. I find a town right on the land I think is mine. I find a man claiming my country under a lease executed with the Indians."

"A legal lease," I pointed out. "General Sheridan said so."

"He didn't say so," Champion declared. "He said he would not interfere. This town is located on my claim, Pete."

Then, knocking the ashes out of his pipe, he smiled again.

"But we can let that lay. About your father, Pete. Tell me your side of the story, please."

"Why?"

"In some matters, Pete," he said dryly, "I can be trusted."

I told him. I told him slowly and reluctantly. His look seemed to pull every word out of me.

He nodded when I had finished. "Thanks, Pete. I've been sure all along that your father wouldn't bushwhack a kid."

"My dad wouldn't bushwhack anybody," I stated.

"Of course not," he agreed. "About this deal of mine with Mulloy," he added, now reluctant to talk in his turn. "We are partners through necessity, Pete. I want this Arapaho country open. Mulloy wants it for cattle. Both of us want the same thing."

"Yeah," I snapped. "Rich Stewart out."

"Rich Stewart out," Champion agreed. His face showed a faint smile. "I'll make a confession, Pete. I can handle Tim Mulloy when the time comes. I can make a deal with him and split the territory up, the north half for him, the south for my company, and when the time comes for settlers to move on into the cattle country, I think I can get Mulloy out. But your partner Rich, he has a dream as grandiose as mine. Mulloy wants a spread, and we can get along for a time. Stewart wants an empire. Two empire builders, or would-be builders, can never get along."

"And that is your deal with Mulloy—you chase Stewart out and split the country up between you?"

"Yes," he admitted calmly.

"That's . . . that's . . ."

I stopped. I couldn't find the words to express myself.

"It would be what you call a grass war," Martin said, "except that I don't want grass."

"You got more gall than gumption," I said hotly. "The law of this country is the six-gun. If you want to jump Rich, do it like a man. Strap your gun on and I'll tell him you want to see him. Don't be hiding here in your cubby-hole every time he comes to town."

His lips tightened. He started to speak once, then caught himself. Finally he said in a strained voice:

"You respected your father, didn't you, Pete?"

"Sure."

"Your father didn't believe in six-gun law

either," Champion murmured. "He didn't believe in settling feuds with a duel."

"But he wasn't scared," I pointed out. "When Mulloy jumped he said he'd wear a gun."

"Stewart has never asked me to put on a gun," Martin reminded me.

"Will you if he does?" I demanded hopefully.

He studied a moment. "No," he said finally, "of course not." He showed that faint smile again. "Technically, perhaps, your friend is the challenged party and should have the choice of weapons. But I can't yield that. I'll have to fight my way."

He turned back to his desk. "And that, Pete," he said stiffly, "might prove to be an effective one. Some of these days your friend Rich might run into an interesting situation when he rides into town."

He swung back to me. "For instance," he murmured, "our new marshal might object to Mr. Stewart's free and easy ways."

"No two-bit marshal is gonna bother Rich," I said scornfully, and stalked out of the building.

I meant it. Where would they get a marshal who was willing to jump on Rich?

Lula Belle had heard the talk that the "mayor" had sent for a marshal. So had all the hangers-on at the saloon.

"That will help business," said one of her dealers. "The boys in on a spree like to make a marshal dance. Maybe they'll build a jail."

Pecos came riding in the next morning. "Rich out of pocket?" he demanded.

"Yes."

Sherrill didn't even dismount, just swung one leg over his saddlehorn as he talked.

"There are a couple of nester families in the lease," he drawled. "What does the boss want done with 'em?"

"I'll ride out with you," I said.

First I went to the hotel for my gun. From now on, I promised myself as I strapped it on, I'd never be without it. Evidently we would have to get rough with these homesteaders who were coming in every day.

In a small valley ten or twelve miles from Cimarron, a mile inside Rich's lease, two Scottish families were toiling away at log houses. They stopped working as Pecos and I rode up. There were five men, three young, the other two obviously family heads. The latter came forward to meet me. Both were bearded grim looking men.

"Howdy," I said curtly.

They bobbed their heads. I could see women peeping out from under the canvas-covered wagons. Three small children were playing around the moss-lined spring.

"Reckon you made a mistake picking this valley," I said coldly. "This is Rich Stewart's country."

"We stopped at the first water we found," the elder of the two men said sullenly. "Reckon we ain't bothering Stewart. Why should he bother us?"

"There is open country south of the river," I pointed out. "Pull up and move over there."

"There ain't water over there," was the defiant answer.

Pecos nudged his horse closer. "Let's go pick up some of the boys," he said, "and scatter these danged hoemen from hell to breakfast."

"No," I said. "We can handle it."

I knew that Rich wouldn't have waited until riders could come up from the main camp. Rich would have acted himself—then.

I jerked out my gun.

"Lift 'em high," I ordered. "And line up."

It was the first time I had ever pointed a gun at a human being. I was shocked to find out how easy it was. The thought struck me as they flinched before the weapon in my hand that perhaps I could hold my own with a Mulloy.

The three younger men were standing stock-still, seemingly stunned by the sight of a gun. I waved for them to line up alongside their fathers.

Then I turned to the wagons and ordered the women out.

Something warned me to look around. I turned just in time to see one of the boys diving for a rifle propped up against the log foundation.

Pecos shot it out of his hand. Blood dripped down the nester's wrist as he sullenly took his place in line and there was no other gesture of resistance made.

"Hitch up the wagons," I ordered the women. They were scared stiff but they moved quickly to obey my orders. One of them was a pretty girl just in her teens, slim and with curly black hair. She spat at me as I waved my gun in her face.

But they got the teams hitched in short order.

"Now start 'em moving," I ordered waving 'em toward town.

The wagons crawled at a snail's pace. It was near dark when we reached Cimarron. I motioned them to pull up in front of Champion's newspaper office. A lamp was burning; Martin was working inside. I called him out without ever dismounting.

I spurred my horse up on the walk by him. They were watching from the saloon, from the hotel, from the homesteaders' camp.

"These friends of yours, Champion," I snapped, "are getting out of line. I found 'em over on our grass."

I turned to the five nester men and pointed out the oldest. "Furthermore," I said, "that man had the gall to sass me. I guess your paper ain't told him yet that this is Rich Stewart's country and nesters had better stay to hell out."

"Lay down that gun," snarled one of the younger men "and we'll . . ."

"Friend," I told him, "we don't lay down our guns. You're lucky it was me who found you instead of Rich Stewart. Rich might have burned your wagons."

One of the women spoke up, the first peep out of them. "Yes," she said bitterly, "I guess this Rich Stewart is that mean."

"Mean, hell!" I snarled at her, not caring if I was talking to a woman. "That's his land. Stay off it and Rich Stewart will tip his hat when he passes you on the street. Or he'll give you a side of beef when your smokehouse is empty. But don't drive your wagons into that country again."

I turned to Champion. "Do you want people killed?" I demanded hoarsely. "Do you think you can run us off? You're new to this country and you may not know that cattlemen hold their ranges. But talk to somebody who does know, Champion, before you get any notions that we're trying to windy."

With that I turned my horse toward the saloon, motioning Pecos Sherrill to follow. I rode close to one of the wagons and the same curly-haired girl stuck her head out from behind the canvas and made a face at me.

"You think you're smart," she jeered.

It was right foolish of me, but I jerked out my gun and sent a shot through the canvas not a yard above her head. She fell back behind the cover with a shriek and I went chuckling on into Lula Belle's.

Pat was still up when I got to the hotel.

"Can't you leave such demonstrations to Rich?" she asked coldly. "I don't like to see my younger brother showing off how tough he is."

"Rich wasn't here," I said curtly. "When he ain't here, I act for him."

She eyed me resentfully. "Why haven't you told me what you've learned about Dad?" she demanded.

"I haven't learned anything," I said, and that was just about the truth.

"I've heard talk," she insisted. "Tim Mulloy has made the statement at that saloon where you hang out that Dad has come into the Cimarron, that he's hiding at Rich's camp."

"I was up there," I pointed out, "and I didn't see him."

"Has Rich seen him?"

"No."

"I don't think Dad would go to Rich for help," she said. "He wouldn't go to anybody."

She leaped up and walked around the room.

"I wish we could find him," she said fiercely, "I wish we could go on to Wyoming or Montana or somewhere, the three of us. Or there are dozens of places we could go to. We have a start. And we could leave all this shooting and hating behind."

I stared at her. "And Rich, too?" I asked softly.

"Why not?" she demanded. "Rich has been a boom country drifter all of his life. Would he ever settle down? If he got his way here, and made his money, would he buy a ranch and build a home and raise a family away from the smell of six-guns and the rush of trail herds?"

"Yes," I said honestly, "I think he would."

"I wish I could think so," she murmured. She sighed. "I don't like his kind of life, Pete. I wish I could, but I can't."

"I suppose," I said unpleasantly, "you like Martin Champion better?"

"I like what he stands for better," Pat answered defiantly. "He doesn't like saloons. You may not know it, young man, but that woman at the honkey-tonk isn't going to stay here long."

"Lula Belle!"

"Yes."

"What's going to happen to her?"

"The city council has passed an ordinance prohibiting gambling," Pat informed me, a cold gleam in her eyes. "How can she keep her place going without gambling?"

I chuckled. "Who is going to enforce it?"

"The new marshal."

I stared at Pat. "The dirty rat," I murmured. I was talking to myself, and the rat I had in mind was Champion. So that was the purpose of this organization of a town and this hiring of a marshal? The guy was more dangerous than I had thought. It was all tying together—the new marshal, Tim Mulloy, Icado's Arapaho followers.

A voice called from downstairs.

"Miss Patricia!"

Her face colored. "Tell Martin I'll be down in a minute, please," she asked me.

She turned to the mirror and started fussing with her hair.

"You letting him spark you?" I demanded.

She tossed her head. "Mr. Champion and I are going for a walk," she snapped. "Is there anything wrong with that?"

I went downstairs. Champion was waiting at the bottom step.

I eyed him coldly. "You'd steal everything a man has, wouldn't you?" I growled.

That faint smile again. "What was it your friend told the General?" he countered in a mild voice. "Wasn't it something about kicking the door open and moving in?

"Besides," he added in the next breath, "I'm breaking no locks, Pete."

I turned around and went back upstairs without delivering the message. I passed Patricia on the way. She acted as if she didn't see me.

# CHAPTER EIGHT

The thousand longhorns came from John Chisum's outfit in the Concho country and Chisum himself bossed the outfit. It thrilled me to talk to this man who had sent as many herds up the trail as any cowman in Texas. Yet it also shocked me to meet him. He was a fleshy little man with a quick laugh and not a sign of a gun on him.

The cows wore a dozen different brands. I started to question 'em, then remembered the yarns about Chisum carrying his powers of attorney in a lead pipe and wrote him out an order without comment.

He asked many a question about Rich. They had never met, though he had sent word to Rich once trying to hire him for a trail boss.

"If he is running short of chips," said the Jingle Bob King, "I'd like a cut on his lease."

I remembered Rich's proposition to Tim Mulloy. "Mebbe he'll get in too deep," I answered. "I'll tell him what you said."

He hurried off with his riders. They had split a herd in the Escano basin and were going to trail the rest to Denver.

I told him good-bye and started back to the hotel. A small crowd of homesteaders were in front of Champion's reading the latest issue of his paper. They seemed to be excited about the contents, so I stopped and bought one. The publisher himself sold it to me.

"Here's an extra copy," Martin Champion said quietly. "Please see that Mr. Stewart gets it with my compliments."

I took the paper and stuck it in my pocket. Opening up my copy, I gasped.

In black type across the front page was:

## SETTLERS READY FOR WAR WITH RICH STEWART!

Three different stories fitted under the banner. One of them had the subhead:

## CITY COUNCIL ASKS APPROVAL OF MULLOY LEASE

I skimmed through the contents.

> A petition signed by the mayor of Cimarron and every member of the council has been sent to General Philip Sheridan requesting a new hearing upon the lease held by Rich Stewart with the Arapaho Indians.
> The mayor and council have unanimously requested that General Sheridan

carefully consider cancelling the Stewart agreement with the Indians and approving the application of Tim Mulloy and Bob Purdy, two other cattlemen, for lease of the Arapaho reservation under the supervision of the Indian agency.

Mulloy, who owns extensive holdings in Texas but is temporarily making his quarters in Cimarron, has offered to open up the south half of the reservation to settlers if his application for a lease is approved.

"There is too much land for any one man," stated the cattleman. "Homesteaders cannot settle on Indian territory but Rich Stewart holds a government lease on 20 sections due south of the reservation. If this lease is canceled, and I can secure it, I will permit settlement on it and also will allow homesteaders to mix their cattle with mine, if branded, on the Arapaho grass."

Walter Jenson, the Arapaho agent, has added his approval to the Mulloy-Purdy lease. The cattlemen propose to pay the agency for the use of the grass and the agency, in turn, will issue additional supplies to the Indians.

"The Arapahos," Jenson said, "are taking the cash Stewart pays them and are buying whiskey with it. Any day now an epidemic of Indian outrages will break out. The Arapahos are quarreling among themselves and their young men are getting ready to go on the warpath."

There was more of that story, all about the same. I turned my grim attention to the others.

## NEW CITY MARSHAL ARRIVES: CLEANUP OF TOWN CERTAIN

I skimmed through the body type. The story read:

> Al Poggin will arrive in Cimarron on the day of this publication to assume his duties as city marshal.
> The mayor of Cimarron will present him immediately upon his arrival his instructions from the city council to immediately close all saloons where gambling is permitted.
> The new marshal is famous over the frontier, having won for himself the name of "Town Tamer" by his exploits at Ellsworth and other boom towns.
> Mr. Poggin seems like the ideal man to represent the law in Cimarron. He will not be afraid to carry the fight right into

the enemy camp. The closing of gambling tables and gaudy saloons is expected to deal a deathblow to the ambitions of Mr. Rich Stewart, the greedy cattleman. It is open talk that Mr. Stewart's cattle ventures are at least partially financed by the woman known as Lula Belle.

I cursed and turned to the third story, reading:

## ARAPAHO OUTRAGES THREATEN PEACE OF CIMARRON

The latest in a series of Indian forays occurred at a village near Cimarron on Sunday night. A handful of Arapaho Indians, all of whom had been drinking, rode boldly up to the house of Rodney Kemp, a settler from Tennessee, and forcibly removed three saddle horses from his stable.

The savages did not molest either Mr. Kemp or his family but threatened to return.

These outrages are not unexpected. Walter Jenson, Arapaho agent, warned General Sheridan against them last month when the military commander held a hearing in Cimarron on the merits of Rich Stewart's lease with the Indians.

"Indians cannot be controlled," Mr. Jenson told the editor of the *Bugle*, "unless we can also control their moneys and issues. As long as the Arapahos are free to spend the gold as they wish, we can expect only the worst."

I wadded up the paper and glared at Champion.

"Do you think you can get by with this?" I demanded hoarsely. "Do you know anything about Mulloy?"

"I've heard things," he admitted quietly.

"And you can team up with a man like that?"

"He promises to open up country to the settlers," he answered. "I want land open for homesteads around Cimarron, Pete. I'll work with any man who offers that."

"They're using you for a tool," I snapped. "Mulloy may want to make money, I dunno about that. But the main thing he wants is to break Rich Stewart and to find my dad."

"I certainly bear your father no malice," Champion said slowly. "Patricia has told me something about—his misfortunes. Mulloy's motive may be hatred. I don't know. It doesn't matter. We agree on one thing . . . to break Rich Stewart."

"I suppose," I sneered, "that you think this new marshal of yours can do it."

"He can close up the Lula Belle," the newspaper man answered quietly. "That will cut off Rich's financial support. Without the revenues from Lula Belle's bar and gambling tables, Rich can't operate another thirty days."

I sighed. He was very close to the truth there.

I turned away from him and went unhappily toward the saloon. One of our riders was loafing there and I sent him for Rich on the double-quick.

Then I went to the hotel to grab a bite.

Champion was eating at the next table with a stranger whom I guessed to be the new marshal even before he opened his coat as he leaned back and I saw the flash of his star.

He was a small fellow in his forties, with thin streaks of gray hair in his head, with deep-set eyes that regarded me with almost a sorrowful look. I couldn't say I was too much impressed.

Patricia came in just then and Champion bowed and she smiled. She seemed to be in a gay mood, as if the loneliness was no longer grating on her nerves. Not until I wolfed my food and pushed back my chair did a shadow cross her face.

"Where are you off to now?" she demanded. "Can't you play a game of seven-up? Or at least talk awhile?"

"I've got to see Lula Belle," I explained. I had decided I should warn her about Champion's intentions.

"The woman at the saloon!"

"Yes."

Her lips set in a firm line. "You're spending

too much time down there, Pete," she reproved me. Then, her voice strained: "You aren't getting interested in a honkey-tonk girl down there, are you?"

"No," I said quickly. "Don't worry about that."

And I meant it. Neither one of us had been raised to be very sympathetic toward Lula Belle's type of woman. No painted floozy she would ever have in her saloon would interest me.

Lula Belle came gliding across the saloon to greet me, but without her usual smile.

"Have you heard from Rich?" was the first thing she asked me.

"Not yet. I sent Steve out for him."

"I wish he'd come," she sighed. "I'm worried. The new marshal is in town."

"I saw him a while ago," I nodded. "Named Poggin."

Lula Belle's full bosom heaved. "I've seen him," she shivered. "He's a demon, Pete. A devil."

"Demon!" I exclaimed. That thin-haired sorrowful-eyed man! What was there about him to put Lula Belle into such a panic!

"He is a fanatic," she went on. "He hates saloons—and women like me—with a deadly passion. And he's cold murder with a six-gun. His son was killed in a saloon fight, or something like that, and he has devoted his life to wiping boom towns off the map. He didn't come here to be just another marshal, Petey. He is here to persecute *me,* and people like me."

She wrung her hands. "He's brutal," she said with a shudder. "He would just as soon shoot me down as—any man. But usually he just pistol-whips the women. I saw what he did—to one girl—in Ellsworth."

"What right does Poggin have to come in and start trouble?" I demanded.

"He is the law," was the dull answer. "My people can't fight back the law, right or wrong."

She sent for a whiskey, the first time I had ever seen her order a glass for herself.

"If it was just me," she mused bitterly, "I'd pull up and move on. But Rich is depending on me. I've got to stick with him."

Somehow she seemed younger and softer when she was worried. She didn't have the usual boldness of manner nor the hard glint in her eyes. As she leaned forward to rest her elbows on the table, I could see entirely too much of her bosom, and I blushed at my consciousness of her lush figure. I couldn't think of calling a woman like her sweet; my notions of a sweet woman were all tied up with hidebound conventions and careful, even severe rearing. But I was beginning to see what Rich meant; Lula Belle was a woman to depend on.

For she was scared, plumb scared. And yet she wasn't about to run.

"Rich will need at least twenty thousand more," she went on in that same absorbed manner. "I could make it for him here—if it wasn't for this Poggin."

I was suddenly bold enough to put a question I had been worrying about for a long time.

"What do you get out of this deal with Rich?" I asked.

She looked at me for a long moment and her expression slowly changed. The worry left her face and suddenly there was a smile on her red full lips, a wistful sort of smile.

"My money back, maybe," she murmured. Then, in a different tone, she added:

"Otherwise, not one damned thing."

Yes, she said it fiercely, even with that smile on her face and that look in her eyes.

She stood up and smiled at me. "Whenever you want something, Petey," she murmured, "go to a honkey-tonk woman for it. They're suckers, every damned one of 'em. They like to think they're making a living out of men. But all they're doing is living *for* men. And, take it from Lula Belle, it ain't such a good way to live."

Then she went toward the bar, swinging her hips, calling out to one of the men to roll high dice with her for the drinks. This man had been hanging around with Tim Mulloy. Probably he was one of the crew Tim was rounding up.

He put his arm around Lula Belle and she

laughed up at him and brushed his cheek with her lips. He threw a goldpiece down on the bar. I chuckled to myself. A lot of the money out of Mulloy's pockets was going to Rich Stewart via this saloon and this woman.

Tim came through the door with his even deliberate pace, saw me, looked off. But not Jeb. Jeb rolled over to my table, his bowed legs even more unsteady because of the whiskey he had been drinking. He smelled heavily of it and there was that looseness about his mouth some men show when they have been drinking.

"How long is your pap going to keep running?" he asked harshly.

I acted as if I didn't hear him.

"We'll get him," boasted Jeb. He caught my arm. "Hear that, button! We'll get him. He bought some things in Seymour night before last."

My heart leaped. Seymour was a town only about twenty miles away.

Suddenly Jeb was spun around by his thin cousin. "Get back to the room, Jeb!" ordered Tim Mulloy. "When you get likkered up you can't keep a halter on your tongue."

Cousin stared at cousin, and there was hatred in their looks.

"Some day, Tim," growled Jeb, "you're going too far."

"And some day," the elder Mulloy snapped, "you're gonna be thrown out on your own. Go back to the hotel and stay there 'til you sober up."

Jeb Mulloy hesitated, then waddled off in obedience. Tim Mulloy watched his cousin out of the saloon, then gave me a quick sidewise look. His lips moved but he turned to the bar without making an audible sound.

Dad in Seymour! I motioned to Lula Belle. She gestured she would join me in a moment.

Then I was conscious of a sudden eloquent quiet. There is nothing as impressive as a honkey-tonk suddenly becoming still. I looked around to see that everybody had frozen in his tracks and that everyone was staring at the door where stood a slight cold-faced man whose hands hung almost to his knees; he had to keep his elbows bent to hold his fingers close to the pearl handles of his guns.

Lula Belle left the bar and came forward slowly.

"What is it?" she demanded.

She was frightened, and if she was trying to hide that fact she was failing miserably. She trembled like a leaf as she stood waiting for Poggin's answer.

The marshal looked past her to the men at the bar, to the girls at the tables, to the piano player on his small stage, to the poker game in the corner, to the roulette table.

Then his blazing eyes settled on Lula Belle.

"Are you running this place?" he demanded.

"Yes," she answered, licking her lips as if they were dry.

I couldn't believe what happened next. I still think back and wonder if my eyes saw aright. For, without a word of warning, Al Poggin whipped out one of his guns and slashed Lula Belle across the forehead with its heavy handle. She dropped in a heap and lay there moaning.

The marshal stepped contemptuously over her.

"I'm closing this place," he announced grimly.

Both guns had leaped quickly into his hands. "Get out," he snarled at the drinkers and the girls and the gamblers, including them all with a nod of his head.

They started moving. They were afraid of him and I didn't blame them. Here was a man who would shoot in cold blood without a qualm of conscience. I have never seen such a terrifying sight as Al Poggin standing there, guns level, shoulders pointed, eyes glowing coals in his awful wrath.

I was scared, too, and I don't deny it. But instead of filing out with the rest of them, I went to Lula Belle, and bent over her and felt of her pulse.

I felt Al Poggin's toe in my ribs, hard, merciless.

"I said get out," snarled the marshal.

"She's hurt," I said defiantly. "I'm gonna take care of her."

I looked up at him and I know I trembled like a cottonwood limb when the north wind hits it. It wasn't so much the fear of being killed—it was the paralyzing fright the gleam of his eyes put into you. He affected you that way, like a snake.

"Who are you?" he demanded.

"I'm Rich Stewart's partner," I managed to say, "and you'll pay for this."

He stared at me. Once his right gun came up slowly. I wanted to draw my own weapon, but his gaze held me paralyzed, helpless. Then, abruptly, he stepped around me and Lula Belle and stalked to the door. He turned back.

"Don't open this place again," he ordered.

And then he pushed his way scornfully through the men falling all over each other in their haste to get outside before him.

I got two of the frightened girls to help me carry Lula Belle to her room. She had a bad cut; for a terrible moment I thought she was dead. Then she opened her eyes and began to moan and I knew she had suffered a bad slash. I washed the cut and stopped its bleeding with lard.

She could sit up now. Blood had stained the front of her rich velvet gown and she was as pale as a ghost. She took her hand mirror and studied the wound and then sobbed out:

"I'll be scarred all of my life."

I had to admit that. This wasn't a deep cut, but the swipe of Al Poggin's gun had left a three-inch abrasion. Yes, Lula Belle, the honkey-tonk queen, would carry this scar to her grave! Always it would be there, just over her eyebrows, ruining the voluptuous majesty of a face and a figure that men had thought about wistfully over their campfires.

"I'm sorry, Lula Belle," I murmured.

She sat up now, rocking back and forth in her chair, every now and then staring at her mirror. I suppose a boy like me couldn't appreciate how much her physical beauty had meant to her. Many things she had abandoned, but never her fierce pride in her own looks. Because of her beauty she had been able to own her own place and to bestow her favors only upon those men she preferred.

Then she stopped rocking, and she looked at me with a smile on her lips, and I felt again that rushing startling admiration for her, that first quiver of a worship for her, even though here, gown askew, one full breast completely bare, she was completely . . . what she was.

"Pete," she whispered, "can I kiss you?"

For a moment I was angry, and the shadow in her eyes showed she realized it. Then I felt a different way entirely. I bent over and tightened my arm around her.

"Shucks, yes," I said with a surprising boldness. "I reckon I'll never get a chance to kiss a prettier woman."

# CHAPTER NINE

Al Poggin walked the streets of Cimarron sternly and alone, and all men shrunk from him. The saloon did not reopen and the girls left for Henderson. The living quarters behind the bar were empty and unkempt as Lula Belle lay in bed with an Indian woman stolidly attending her. Her sickness was more mental than physical. Nothing interested her.

It was a quiet town. Pecos Sherrill brought news that Rich had gone to the Arapaho camp for another powwow with Catamo. The handful of riding men who had drifted in and had promptly been put on Mulloy's pay roll were off somewhere, Tim and Jeb with them. I didn't have to guess where they were, and rumors floated back to confirm my suspicion. They were scouring the country between here and the trading store at Seymour, and my dad was the quarry.

I wanted Rich to come in something awful. These were a miserable few days. Something ought to be done about a couple of things, about Lula Belle and about Dad.

The only people circulating were the nesters. Nathan Stool's store did a rushing business. A doctor arrived in town and the Scots quickly threw him up a small office. He ate in the hotel, a clean-cut chap, quickly the best of friends with Martin Champion.

"What's his handle?" I asked Pat, referring to the doctor.

"Dr. Randolph Moore," she said promptly. "He's nice, isn't he?"

"He looks plumb purty," I sneered.

I hadn't told her what I had learned about Dad. She was even more helpless than I was. The lone man hiding in this wild country had to work alone.

I wandered from the saloon to the office to the hotel and back again. If I could get him food and water and shells and money, he might make out. He could ride and he was smart in the open. In every way except with a six-gun Dad could hold his own with any man in the west.

Champion called out to me on one of those miserable walks.

"Worried about something, Pete?" he asked.

His tone seemed kindly but I couldn't be sure. Probably he had heard rumors about my dad; Jeb had talked plenty.

"I'm *bueno*," I said curtly.

He studied me a minute, then shut off talk with a nod.

Three days passed. Tim Mulloy rode back into Cimarron with his cousin and two bearded followers. They bought provisions at Stool's and ate in the same dining room with us at the hotel. I couldn't touch a bite of my food. It made me sick to look at 'em and to think I couldn't do anything about them.

But it was plain from the dust on their faces and their ill-humor that Frank Haines hadn't been trapped yet. For that I could be grateful.

I left my pie untouched and offered no explanation to Patricia for this strange act. A copy of Champion's latest paper lay on the round table. I was looking at it when Luke Martin came up behind me.

"Letter for you, Pete," Luke whispered and thrust something in my hand.

I didn't open it at once. Tim Mulloy could see me through the open partition, though he didn't seem to be paying me any mind. Luke's tone indicated secrecy. I jammed the paper in my clenched fist and ducked up to my room.

There was no envelope, only a folded sheet of paper. On it was written:

> Don't worry about me, Pete. I'm all right. I'm where Tim Mulloy can never find me until I want to see him.

It was signed simply "Dad."

I felt like turning a handspring and rocking the hotel with wild yells.

But I managed to act pretty calm. I went to the

steps and called to Patricia. Behind a shut door I showed her the note.

Her eyes and face lit up at once. She handed the note back to me and I started to burn it. Suddenly she snatched it out of my hand.

"Let me see that again," she cried.

"Pete, it isn't . . . !" she exclaimed after a second examination of the message. She caught herself. She gave me a funny look.

"It isn't what?" I demanded.

She laughed softly. "Nothing. Here, I'll hold it for you. Strike the match."

And the note went swiftly up in flames. Pat hugged me.

"I'm so happy, Pete," she whispered. "I'm sure of it for the first time . . . Dad is safe in the Cimarron."

"I feel better, too," I admitted. "He says he is in a safe place. Reckon that means he has gotten to Rich's camp."

"Maybe," she said in a funny tone.

I went downstairs. I couldn't sit still, but it was a different kind of restlessness than that which had nearly driven me crazy the last few days. I wanted to laugh in Tim Mulloy's face as I walked by the dining room where they were still eating. But I didn't.

I fought against the temptation to tell Lula Belle. I could trust her, I was sure of that. But, I cautioned myself, the fewer who knew about it, the better. I decided not to even tell Rich that the note had been received.

Walking up the street, feeling high after being so low, I came face to face with one of the young nesters I had driven off Rich's lease at the point of a gun. With him was the slim curly-haired girl who had made a face at me, and who had dived back into her wagon when I had shot over her head.

The nester was bigger than I by a full head and several years older.

The girl spoke first.

"Well, if it isn't Mister High-and-Mighty!" she jeered.

I pretended not to notice her. But the nester snarled something that began with a "damn" and I whirled on him.

"If you want trouble," I said coldly, "you can have it."

He was a big stooped youth in his twenties at least. He looked back at me sullenly.

"Like I told you that day," he growled, "if you lay down that gun . . ."

Like a fool I did it.

"Beat him up, Beanie," shrieked the girl as the nester dived at me.

I hit him with a right but it didn't phase him. He must have outweighed me by forty pounds, for he broke through my guard with his bull rush and seized me around the waist and bore me to the ground. I knew it would be rough on me if he ever got me down. I swung a knee into him and he groaned, but it didn't stop him. His hands were like hams; one of them hit me in the mouth and I saw stars and tasted salty blood.

All of the time the nester girl was screaming and a crowd was gathering.

I was down. And the hoeman wasn't going to just let me up. He sat on my chest and smashed with both hands.

Then I felt his weight jerked off me. Martin Champion stood there, his face furious. He slapped the nester and sent him spinning with a push.

Then he helped me to my feet.

"Are you all right, Pete?" he asked anxiously.

"I guess so," I grunted. My head was still ringing but I wasn't conscious of any permanent injury.

The newspaper man turned back to the scowling nester. "You should be ashamed of yourself," he scolded. "You're a bully in the first place. In the second, you started a brawl. We'll hold the first city court in Cimarron in the morning. You be at my office at eight o'clock prepared to face charges."

"Yes, Mister Champion," the hulking youth muttered.

Champion looked around him grimly. "We won't levy fines in my court," he announced.

"Every family needs their hard cash too badly. But offenders like Beanie here will work out their fine on the town streets at $1 a day."

I wiped the blood from my face and caught the mayor's shoulder.

"Wait a minute," I protested. I had learned a little about law from my schoolteacher in the Frio. "I didn't claim this man jumped me. I had as much to do with starting the fight as he did."

"He's so much bigger," Champion frowned.

"What's his fine?" I demanded, reaching into my pocket. I wasn't like the nester boys; I had money there.

"Do you intend to pay it?" he shot back.

"I sure do," I said firmly.

His lips quirked. "Ten dollars for the both of you," he said. "Do you want the sentence in court or do you want it here?"

"I'll take it here," I snapped. I pitched two ten-dollar goldpieces toward him.

He caught them. He studied them a moment, then looked at me. His face was still grim but there was approval in his eyes.

"Court dismissed," he said dryly.

I limped to the hotel, washed my face and doctored my cuts and bruises. Next time, I thought ruefully, I wouldn't be so danged proud. I'd hang on to my gun.

Then I went down to see how Lula Belle was feeling. Her head still ached like the dickens, she said, but otherwise she was *bueno*. But she was lying in bed as if she didn't give a damn whether she lived or not. She had been lying like that for five days.

I walked around the back of the saloon and toward the crowd. I could see some of the Scots milling around in front of Nathan Stool's store, still buying supplies on the credit. I had heard Nathan explain why he would give credit to any homesteader.

"My store, it vill grow," said the Jewish trader. "You owe me, you pay later. Ve have people here ready to move. My store, it vas here first. You remember your goot friend, Nathan. It's business, goot business."

I watched them bitterly. Could it be possible, I thought, that one gun-slick marshal could run us out of the country?

Then, as I turned back toward the corral, I saw the chestnut coming up the dusty side road, its sides covered with sweat and dirt. Others turned to watch as Rich Stewart swung out of his saddle in front of the hotel. I saw Al Poggin standing across the street, eyes staring at Rich's back. The marshal was picking his teeth with a sharpened match end and there was the same melancholy look in his eyes I had noticed in the hotel.

I called to Rich and he waited for me. Then, as his eyes swept the street, he saw Al Poggin and recognized the marshal. Rich's body lost its lazy sag and his features hardened.

"When did Poggin get here?" was the first thing he asked me.

"The other day. And he has already pistol-whipped Lula Belle and closed down her saloon."

"How is she?" he demanded anxiously.

"*Bueno*. But she'll carry a scar on her forehead. It was an ugly cut."

I looked back at Poggin, who hadn't stirred. "He came into the saloon, Rich, and everybody was scared stiff," I babbled. "He conked Lula Belle without saying a word. When I tried to help her, he kicked me. But I didn't let him run me out like he did everybody else, Rich. I stayed there and took care of her."

His hand gripped my shoulder. "Sure you did," he murmured. "I don't worry about things when you're around, pardner."

Then he hitched his belt. "Come along, Pete," he grunted. "We need a drink. Me especially. Need to wash the dust out of my throat."

"Where can we get one?" I demanded. "Lula Belle has shut down. Most of the other honkey-tonk people have run off to Henderson."

His lips parted, showing his teeth.

"We'll drink at Lula Belle's," he murmured.

We walked slowly toward the saloon. Martin Champion stood in front of his office, his white shirt front gleaming as he was surrounded by

Scots in their dark homespun. None of them spoke as we walked by.

We reached the front of the locked saloon and Rich stopped to roll a cigarette.

"Go around to Lula Belle's room," he said. "Tell her she's got a customer."

Before I could utter the protest that formed on my lips, that it was sheer suicide to face Al Poggin, my excited feet were carrying me around to the back entrance. I found Lula Belle in bed, a wet cloth over her battered face. When I told her what Rich had said, she threw back the cover and fairly leaped up. She wore only a thin nightgown and in the broad open daylight she might as well have worn nothing at all.

But she didn't stop to pull on a kimono or anything. She walked through the back door into the saloon with me following her. She threw open the front door and she stood there framed in the rush of daylight. Except for the bandage on her head, she might have been a woman on the front of a calendar. But I doubt if any of the gawking men even noticed the bandage.

"Why, come in, Rich," she called out. "Come right in."

He was standing right by the door and there was no call for her to speak out so loud. But, of course, she wanted her voice to float down the street to where Martin Champion and the nesters were watching, and farther on to where Al Poggin still stood picking his teeth.

"Come in," she called again. "The first drink is on the house."

And, breasts dancing under her thin gown, she went behind the bar to pour the drink herself.

Rich leaned against the bar, his face grim. He didn't look at Lula Belle, nor at me when I joined him.

"Hurt, honey?" he asked in a low voice.

"Just a gash," she shrugged. "What will you have, Pete?"

"The same as Rich," I answered.

She poured the drinks. Then she stood studying Rich's face.

"You can't beat him, Rich," she said gently. "You know that, don't you?"

He didn't answer.

"I saw him in Ellsworth," went on Lula Belle. "You're good yourself, Rich. But Poggin practices all the time. That's his whole life."

He inclined his head slightly.

"I know it," he murmured.

That came as a shock to me. Not until that moment had I been afraid for Rich Stewart. I had been so sure that Rich could outshoot any man in the world that I hadn't stopped to consider that Poggin had a reputation of his own, and that from the way men shrunk away from the thin-haired marshal it must be deserved.

I caught Rich's shoulder. I couldn't stand there and be as calm about it as Lula Belle. For, two blocks down the street, Al Poggin had thrown away his crude toothpick and was walking slowly toward the open saloon door.

"Rich, dang it!" I protested. "If you can't handle the man, let him . . ."

He shrugged off my hand. "He'll hit me," he said in a dull tone. "But maybe I'll get one shot."

"Rich, don't be a fool!" I pleaded.

"Stand back, Pete," he snapped. It was the first and last time he ever spoke to me in an ugly tone. Then, noticing the look on my face, a grin split his lips.

"Sorry, pardner," he drawled.

And then, his left hand flopping at his side, his right arm tense and curved at the elbow, he stepped out of the saloon.

I watched in horrified fascination. Poggin stopped a hundred feet away and the two men stared at each other, both of them squinting, as if seeing an extra foot might mean the difference between life and death.

It seemed incredible to me that they could stand there like that, motionless for the moment, but each ready to strike. Not a word had passed between them, not a personal gesture. But Al Poggin had come walking down the street to kill Rich Stewart and Rich had stepped out of Lula Belle's to meet him.

I saw men scurrying to get out of the line of fire. Something clamped my arm in a deathlike grip.

"Hold me, Pete," begged Lula Belle. "Don't let me make a fool out of myself—trying to stop him."

I tried to reassure her but my lips wouldn't utter a word. Now I could see Rich's profile, lean and grim. "God," I said to myself, "go on and get it over with."

But each of these men wanted the other to make the first motion. I suppose that was their pride. There was something, I thought, a little childish about all of this. Something out of the books I had read flitted through my mind. "Fire first, gentlemen of France. Nay, gentlemen of England, the first volley is yours."

There . . . Poggin's hand dipped. My eyes shifted quickly to Rich. But no gaze could follow the movements of either man. It seemed to me that the marshal's gun was first. There was a roar.

There was another.

The smoke billowed up in a cloud. I ran right into it. For it seemed to me that Al Poggin had thrown the first shot.

Yes, Rich was wavering back and forth, gripping his right shoulder. His gun lay flat in the dust at his feet.

"Rich!" I yelled catching his other shoulder.

"*Bueno*, pardner," he murmured throwing an

arm around me and using me as a support. "I waited him out. I got him."

Sure enough Al Poggin was on his knees clawing out with one hand at the thin empty air. Then the man who had shown no mercy toward saloon men and the honkey-tonk women, who had lived for his hatred of them, slipped forward slowly until he reached the dust. Before he died the fierceness left his eyes and the everyday melancholy returned. He didn't look like he had been a formidable man as he lay still in the dust.

Rich was hit in the right shoulder. He walked into Lula Belle's with my help and sat up while we bandaged his wound. He hugged Lula Belle with his good arm.

"My only chance was to make him hurry," he grinned. "I spotted him the first shot."

So that had been the cause of the waiting, a duel of nerves. And Al Poggin had yielded first.

Lula Belle flung open wide the doors of her saloon and, still in her nightgown, shouted for everybody to come in for the first drink on the house. Then she ran to her room. In a moment she was back wearing a flame-red dress.

There were only two men beside Rich and myself, pilgrims both. But the word would get out. The girls and the gamblers would come back and Cimarron would boom again with the glitter cowmen loved to find at the end of the trail.

Lula Belle left us to send an Indian over to

Henderson to tell the girls to return. Rich asked me about Dad.

I stared at him. "You blamed waddy, you know good and well I heard from him," I protested. "I got the note all right."

"What note?" he countered.

"Didn't you send it in—to Luke?"

His head tilted. I explained. He shook his head.

"I heard some talk," he admitted. "Tim Mulloy was beating the brush around our southwest fence. Your dad was spotted in Seymour."

My heart fell. I had been so sure Dad was with Rich.

"But I wouldn't worry, pardner," Rich comforted me. "Frank Haines can take care of himself. It will take more than Tim Mulloy to outsmart him."

I nodded. I could count on that. But I would have felt better if I had known Dad was in Rich's country, with Rich's riders behind him if trouble came.

"Mosey down to the hotel and tell Luke I want a special steak," Rich suggested. "Another drink and I'll be a plumb hungry man."

I obeyed. But I didn't rush right on to the hotel. For my way led by Champion's office and the editor was writing at his desk and I couldn't pass without a taunting remark.

"Know any more two-bit marshals?" I jeered.

He laid down his pen and looked at me gravely. "No, Pete," he said softly. "I don't know any more. I wouldn't send for them if I did."

The way he took it surprised me. And took all the fun out of ribbing him.

"I never saw anything like it," he murmured. "I had heard about gun fights. But I didn't dream that Rich Stewart would ride into town and take up the challenge like that. They said Poggin was unbeatable, Pete. They said . . ."

His voice fell off. He shrugged his shoulders and a faint smile came to his face.

"I learn things about this country every day, Pete," he admitted.

"It's too rough for the likes of you," I advised him, and I wasn't meaning to be nasty.

"In some ways," he conceded. Then, squaring back his shoulders, showing that quirk to his lips again: "In some ways I'm rough, too, Pete. I'm not through yet. I'm profiting by my mistakes."

Dennis Cameron stepped into the office just then. He looked at me without a greeting, then said to Champion:

"You want to see me, Mister Champion?"

"Yes, Dennis. Excuse us, Pete."

"Sure," I said. And I guess I swaggered out of the little newspaper office. My kind had won another round.

I delivered the message to Luke and he agreed.

"I'll fill that waddy up to his gills," he declared.

I went back to the saloon after Rich. Passing the newspaper office, I noticed that Stool and the doctor were in there with Champion. And another man, whose back was to me. I stopped. Champion's voice floated out, clear and loud.

". . . We have to gamble the future of our colony. That is the only way Stewart can be handled. I'm sure of it."

"I dunno about that," said the man with his back to the window. I knew him when he started talking. Jenson, the Indian agent. "Icado is ready to challenge Catamo. Maybe the General . . ."

"We tried that," Champion interrupted. "We'll keep on trying it. But I saw Stewart charm General Sheridan once and I'm afraid he can again. Let's make out a list of all the relatives, friends and acquaintances back East. I'll take the letters. . . ."

I walked on with a chuckle. What were they up to now? One thing about Champion, I mused, he was a stubborn cuss. An ordinary man would have given up after watching Al Poggin fall.

Rich said he was ready to eat and I walked back with him.

"They're powwowing in there," I told him as we passed the paper office.

He grunted. We passed by the square of wagons where the supper fires of the homesteaders were sputtering.

"Fixed up real cozy, ain't they?" Rich murmured.

"Yeah," I said bitterly. I could see the girl who had been with the nester youth called Beanie when we fought.

"You had a little ruckus with one of 'em, didn't you?" Rich asked.

"I bit off more than I could chew," I admitted.

"Use your gun on 'em," Rich said curtly. "When you don't shoot, pistol-whip. Don't worry about giving 'em a fair chance. They don't give you one."

Suddenly he chuckled. "Those thousand head of two-year-olds we got cooped up," he said. "Ain't it cruel to keep 'em locked in a corral? They wanna stir around a little and stretch their legs. Will you turn 'em out for me, pardner?"

I stared at him. Was he crazy! It would take us two days to round those steers up again!

"Steers are nosy critters," he continued. "I've seen 'em bump over pots and stomp into campfires."

I caught on. I ran toward the corral hollering for Arch Witherspoon.

We threw open the gates and prodded a few steers out. They came out suspiciously. They were trail-broken and some of their spirit crushed. They milled around uncertainly for a few minutes before the first wondering animal took advantage of his unexpected freedom and began looking for a grassy spot. Then tails swishing and hoofs clattering, the cows began to mosey along the flat. One of 'em approached a homesteader's wagon and was hit by a hail of clods.

The beast wheeled and bolted—right into another wagon.

The vehicle was overturned, and fell atop a cook fire. The canvas blazed up quickly. Women and children screamed. Men rushed forward to fight the fire, yelling hoarsely, cursing angrily.

Arch and I went on to the hotel. We could watch as well from the bench before the entrance. Rich was sitting there laboriously attempting to roll a cigarette with his left hand. I gave him a jump.

The excitement in the nester camp had reached the panic stage as the steers floundered around among the wagons. Another was overturned. Many a kettle full of water or soup or stew went crashing over with a hissing sound.

Martin Champion came up, almost running.

"Stewart, isn't this carrying things too far?" demanded the publisher. "Those poor people are not on your land."

"I'm not bothering 'em," Rich shrugged.

"But your cows certainly are," stormed Martin. "This is a fight between men, Stewart. Must women and children suffer?"

Rich puffed on his cigarette a moment without answering. "Reckon, Champion," he said finally, "that goes with living in a cow country. Like some other things I could mention."

"It's a dirty trick," Champion said hotly.

"Kinda low," nodded Rich. "But not as low as giving whiskey to the Indians."

Martin Champion stared at him. "Is that an accusation?" he demanded through tight lips.

"Don't sabbe your talk too well," Rich shrugged. "I said you or your running mates are keeping Icado in firewater."

"I deny any part in it," Champion said hotly.

"Could be," Rich conceded. "But in this country, friend, we figger a man to be as good or as bad as the outfit he rides with."

Champion studied him. "The day you supply me with proof of any man giving whiskey to the Indians," he promised, "I'll print it in my paper, regardless of who it is."

Rich seemed to think this pledge of no importance, for he ignored it. "I heard your paper was going again," he grinned. Then he pushed back his flop-brimmed hat.

"Noticed you had an ad in it," he drawled. "Got any space to sell for the next issue, Champion?"

"For what?"

"A little speech I'm making for the benefit of some homesteaders and some citizens of Cimarron."

"I'll print that for nothing," Martin snapped. "My paper will always print both sides."

He took a pencil out of his pocket. "All right," he nodded. "I'll quote you, Mister Stewart."

Rich took the pencil and paper and handed it to me. "Write this down, Pete," he said. "We'll pay Champion to print it just like we say."

"You insist it be run as an advertisement?"

"Yep," Rich nodded. "I want it printed in my style."

Martin shrugged his shoulders and motioned for me to write down what Rich said.

"To any hoeman who has any notion of homesteading in the country I have leased," Stewart said slowly. "That is my grass and I know how to keep it. If you take your women and kids into my country, what happens to them is on your head, not mine."

He nodded to me that that was all. He took a twenty-dollar goldpiece and handed it to Champion.

"Reckon that will take care of it."

"You have some change coming," answered the publisher, reaching into his pocket and pulling out a leather purse.

"Keep the change," shrugged Rich.

Champion counted out silver and bills and extended it to Rich.

"I said keep it," Stewart snapped. "Rich Stewart doesn't deal in two-bit stuff."

Martin stared at him a moment, then, with a sweep of his hand, sent the money flying over the walk.

"There it is," he snapped. "You may be needing that money before long, Stewart. For the price of a meal."

# CHAPTER TEN

Champion left town the next morning. But first he held a big confab at his office. All of the people siding with him were there, even Tim Mulloy. Then he came back to the hotel, packed his valise and stopped at the desk to tell Luke he would be gone for a few weeks.

"But hold my room," the newspaper man said. He might have been talking for our benefit, for Rich and I were sitting right there and Champion looked once in our direction. He turned from Luke and walked slowly toward us. He stood looking down at us, and Rich sat looking up at him, and there was no sign of an expression on either face.

"Could I have a word with you, Mister Stewart?" he asked after a moment, his voice cool but not hostile.

"Shoot," Rich agreed.

"If you'll walk outside with me . . ." Champion suggested.

Rich got up lazily. He sauntered after Champion. They walked across the street, Champion a few steps ahead. They stopped under a dust-streaked cottonwood and talked. I watched closely, as curious as all get-out. What could Rich and Champion have to talk about? And Rich was nodding his head again and again.

Then Champion walked briskly toward the livery stable and Rich started back to the hotel. He stopped, as if thinking something over, then turned and went to Lula Belle's.

Pat had come downstairs. "Maybe you can untangle this," I said to her. "Champion and Rich just palavered in private like they were old compadres. Last night they were about to jump down each other's throats. Rich put it to Champion straight that somebody was giving firewater to the Indians. Champion didn't like it one bit. Now they just got through clucking like old women."

"Did they?" Pat asked in mild curiosity. There was a gleam in her eyes.

"What do you know about this?" I demanded.

"Nothing," she answered quickly. "Neither takes me into his confidence."

And she buried her face in a book.

I waited a moment, then demanded: "Where did this Champion light a shuck to?"

"Back East. Kentucky, I believe."

"What for?"

"Why are you so interested in Champion?" she asked looking up.

"The guy is up to something," I grumbled. "They've been holding powwow."

"It's no secret," she said. "Martin is very interested in the presidential election. He is working for Grover Cleveland."

Cleveland, Cleveland! I remembered something about Cleveland. What was it? Oh, yes, Martin telling that Kansas lawyer that something or other depended on Cleveland.

"What does he know about making a president?" I scoffed.

She closed her book. "There are other things in the world, Pete," she said coldly, "besides cattle and honkey-tonks."

With that she went upstairs, walking stiffly. I looked after her sadly. It was getting plainer and plainer to see that Patricia didn't like the prospect of teaming up with a man like Rich. I could stand the idea of that all right. In fact, it struck me that with as many things as Rich and I had to do, a woman would just be in the way anyhow. But she was getting more and more impressed with this Champion. That I didn't like.

Rich came back to the hotel on the double-quick. The news was bad as usual, so bad that I didn't get to drop a hint that I was curious about his confab with Champion.

"More trouble with the Arapahos," he explained tersely. "I gotta get back out to camp."

He agreed to let me go along. I dashed upstairs for a change of socks. Coming by the desk, I saw a letter for Rich on the counter. I handed it to him in the livery stable.

"Don't you ever pick up your mail?"

"Read it to me," he said.

"Hey, wait a minute," I said as he vaulted into the saddle. "This has gotta be answered first."

For it was from General Sheridan.

> Dear sir: I view with alarm the increasing number of disturbances among the Arapaho Indians. You are invited to appear at Fort Sill on or before the first of the month to answer complaints that the activities of your cattle company are contributing to the unrest.

"Damn!" Rich said unhappily.

"I'll write him a letter," I proposed, "and tell him you'll be in to see him next week."

"Next week!" he frowned.

"You got to go, Rich."

"I'll wait for you," he agreed.

It hurt him to have to wait for anybody or anything.

We rode hard though I pointed out to Rich that he shouldn't risk breaking the blood clot in his shoulder wound. We reached the camp in mid-afternoon. Pecos, who was acting as cookie again, greeted us with a wagging of his head.

"I was going to ride in for you tonight, Rich," he said. "I can't hold the boys much longer. Icado run off a bunch of our steers last week and Curly got winged in a running fight with 'em last night."

"Learn anything about where they're getting whiskey?"

"Somebody is slipping it to 'em for sure," shrugged Pecos, "but we can't put a finger on him. This Icado, he's going to make plenty of trouble, Rich. He talks English and he's bragging around that he aims to run us out of here. The boys won't stay, Rich. They know Indians. If you'll lead 'em in a raid on Icado's village, or against Mulloy's crew, they'll settle that redskin's hash and Mulloy's, too. But they ain't gonna put up with this poaching and ambushing."

I looked at Rich hopelessly. I couldn't say that I blamed our riders. There was never any wisdom of fighting a defensive battle against the Indians. One good bloody fight, if carried to their own village, would convince 'em for a spell. But just standing off . . . firing only when fired upon! That was playing the red man's own game.

"I know it's plain hell," admitted Rich, "but that's what we got to do."

We rode around looking until the boys came into camp. The grass was still high, our cows hadn't made an impression on it.

"They've had a rain recently," observed Rich.

We had had only a slight sprinkle and the usual autumn thunderstorms at Cimarron. But here it had rained a-plenty. The cows were fat and they would drop a lot of calves. Rich's eyes gleamed whenever we rode upon a bunch of 'em feeding in a flat.

"Dang it, Pete," he growled, "if I can just get by this winter, I'll be on easy street. Just one winter."

I nodded. I knew what he had paid for those cattle and just about what they were worth now.

We got back to camp just after dark. The boys were waiting, sullen, defiant. Rich started talking. Curly, who was nursing his wounded shoulder, interrupted him with a curse.

"Stow the gab, Rich. If you weren't a right guy, we would have pulled out. You need new hands all around."

"Except for me," Pecos put in with a glare around him.

"Except for Pecos," shrugged Curly. "The rest of us don't cotton to this job."

"Let me finish," Rich said meekly. I knew that was just a temporary act with him—that meekness. I knew no man would ride off from his job without having to settle with Rich. He wasn't about to give up.

He explained his position, which they had heard before. He would go to Icado, the rebellious chieftain, and make a separate treaty for grazing rights to that part of the reservation Icado claimed.

"I know the work is dangerous," he said slowly. "I told you that before we came up here. I thought

I had picked out men who weren't too worried about their own hides."

"We can take our chances as well as the next man," growled Curly, "if we get paid for it."

"So that's what you want?" snapped Rich. "More money?"

"We'd think about it for more money," Curly said defiantly. "And for cash, Rich. We've been thinking some. You're getting your backing from that lady friend of yours. She almost got chased out of town last week. What if she folds up on you? Where are we left?"

Rich's eyes flashed and I thought for a moment he would draw on Curly then and there. But he held his temper, which shows how much it meant to him to keep these men pacified. It was the first time I ever knew Rich Stewart to take anything from anybody.

He studied a moment. "I'll pay a hundred bucks bonus for you to stick out the winter," he proposed.

"Tobacco money," snorted Curly. "Make it three hundred."

Rich refused. They finally settled for two hundred.

"Cash," Curly insisted.

Rich frowned. "Did you expect me to bring six thousand dollars with me?" he demanded.

"Nope," Curly shrugged. Evidently all of the cowboys, except Pecos, had agreed to let this wounded man act as their spokesman. "But you can go back for it. Or send the button there."

"I'll go," I offered, glaring at Curly.

"I'm taking you up, Curly," Rich said softly. "But first I got something to say."

His gaze went from man to man before he spoke again. "I'm gonna pay you," he said slowly. "I don't mind admitting that it's gonna cramp me to do it. But I'm meeting your terms. Then you're gonna meet mine. You're gonna work these cows from dawn to dark. You'll do just what shooting you have to, and that means if you got a chance to run for it, you fan the breeze. You'll stay here 'til spring and the first man who pulls out or who tries to work a fast one is gonna settle with me personally."

He waited a second, then added: "I'll gun the man who doesn't keep his word with me," he promised grimly, "if I hafta follow him to hell and back to do it."

"We told you we'd stick," Curly muttered, his face red. "We mean it."

"*Bueno*," nodded Rich. "Pete, you ride in tomorrow and get the six thousand."

He didn't have to tell me who to turn to for it. Lula Belle, of course.

I nodded.

"Now, boys," grinned Rich in a sudden change of mood, "now that the powwow is over, let's have a drink. I got a saddlebag full of the best whiskey in the Cimarron."

"That's more like it," beamed Pecos.

In two hours' time, they were singing in loud off-key voices and telling jokes punctuated with hearty slaps and loud laughs. That was their way. Their minds were made up when Rich came and he couldn't budge 'em without meeting their terms. But now, the argument over, they were saddle partners again.

The next morning I rode back alone. Rich said he would stay around camp for a few days, then ride over to Fort Sill and confer with Sheridan.

Lula Belle's head wound had nearly healed but the jagged scar had done to her face what she had feared—stripped her of her beauty. Her hair had been her pride and joy; now, with the red scar just underneath, it was an eerie sight, one redder than the other. It was hard to look at her without staring at that scar.

I told her about the trouble at camp and Rich's need for six thousand dollars to pay his thirty riders the advance bonus he had promised. She sighed and showed me a draft drawn upon her Kansas bank for eight thousand. A trail herd had come in from North Texas the night before and she had paid off the straw boss.

"I haven't got it, Pete. Business has been off since Poggin came. It'll pick up again, but not all at once."

"What do I do now!" I exclaimed.

"Won't the boys wait?"

"No," I said unhappily.

I suddenly snapped my fingers. Why hadn't I thought of it before?

"I've got six thousand," I exclaimed. "Pat and I have together, that is. We can spare it."

Sure we could. We hadn't broken a single one of the big bills we had brought from Texas.

Lula Belle's lips tightened.

"Will your sister let you use it like that?"

I hesitated. It was true that she was showing a prejudice against Rich's deal.

"Sure she will," I said.

If not, I told myself, we'd split up. Half of the money was mine and I could use it as I blamed well please.

But Patricia quickly acceded.

"I'm glad to do it," she said.

She got the money out of her valise. She had not asked why Rich needed it, I suddenly thought.

"I want to ride out with you to take it, Pete," she surprised me by saying. "I want to give it to Rich myself."

"Why?"

Her eyes met mine squarely. "We have some other things to talk over, Rich and me," she murmured.

I could guess what she meant. "Like a broken engagement?" I demanded.

"Yes."

She did not flinch before the accusation in my eyes. She met my glance, then said in an even voice: "Wait downstairs for me."

It didn't take her long. I had to hand it to Pat for that; she could rig herself up to look better in less time than any woman I knew. We got away from Cimarron in plenty of time to make Rich's camp by sundown and Pat listened and watched with interest while I described the lay of the Arapaho country.

We rode along easily, interested in our comparisons of this with the Frio country.

Then, ahead of us, we sighted the Arapaho party.

Patricia saw them first, mere specks on the horizon. "Look, Pete!"

My first idea was that they might be Pecos Sherrill and one of our fence crews. But I soon was sure otherwise; an Indian and a cowboy rode in different styles.

"Those are Arapahos," I guessed.

Her eyes showed her quick fright. "They're supposed to be friendly. But aren't some of them . . ."

"Yes," I answered curtly, "they are. If they're Icado's bunch, we're in for it."

And I was pretty sure they were Icado's warriors. The other Arapaho chieftains kept their hunting parties off Rich's lease as they had agreed.

And they had seen us; I could tell that by the way they pulled up, then split into two parties. One group got between us and the trail to Rich's camp, the other circled behind us.

"We'll try to bluff it out," I said desperately.

I didn't see anything else to do. We couldn't fight. I had my rifle and gun, but what was one man against them?

And, I dared to hope, they wouldn't harm us. One or two shooting scrapes between Rich's men and Icado's braves didn't mean that the Arapaho chieftain was taking the warpath in wide-open daylight. If the worst came to the worst, I thought swiftly, remembering the bills in Patricia's saddlebags, we could buy our way through.

The party in front of us now turned and rode slowly in our direction, head-on. They didn't spread out to charge nor did they kick their mounts into a gallop, which was encouraging.

But the Indians behind us came up faster. I had a good horse under me and might have gotten away in a run for it, but Pat's mount was a livery stable nag which was already winded. Twice we had stopped to let the animal breathe and water.

Now the Arapahos ahead pulled up and waited for us. They had the trail squarely blocked. There was no point in our turning off. We kept riding until right upon them; then I raised my hand in greeting and said "how" as calmly as I could.

An Indian pushed his horse forward, some

sort of a sub-chief, I reckon, for he spoke with some authority. He waved his hand around him. I couldn't make out a word of his talk.

Now the red men came up behind us and we were completely surrounded. There were twenty or more of them, with no war paint on their faces and bodies but with rifles and tomahawks and one of them wore a scalp at his belt. Under different conditions I might have snickered at the way they were dressed. Nearly every one of them wore some discarded white man's gear—a hat, a shirt, a pair of trousers, though not a one was completely dressed.

Evidently there were two sorts of chiefs of just about equal authority, for one warrior from the group behind us came up and there was a two-way argument.

I tried to push forward to join the conference but an Arapaho caught my bridle and his intent was unmistakable.

We were prisoners!

I looked helplessly at Pat. Except for a twitching of her lips and the wideness of her eyes, she was not showing her fright.

I tried to talk to the warriors but they only looked at me with solid resentment.

Now one of the two chiefs seized Pat's bridle and jerked her horse forward. Two warriors grabbed at my reins.

I tried to get closer to Patricia but they

wouldn't permit it. A half-dozen warriors rode between us, as many on each side. All of them, I noted, carried rifles, many of them new-looking guns. And most of them had ammunition belts filled with cartridges. Someone, I thought, was supplying guns and shells to these savages.

Once, in the distance, we saw two riders who must have been heading for Rich's main camp. But they were too far away to see any kind of a desperate signal, and besides, when they sighted us they turned and rode rapidly in the opposite direction. They were, I groaned, carrying out Rich's orders.

It was twilight when we were led into the Arapaho village. We had ridden at least twelve miles from the point where the savages had intercepted us; we were not, I figured over ten miles from Rich's camp. None of the warriors had mistreated us in any way, not even binding us, but as we rode through the line of tepees and lodges, we were spat upon, hit with sticks and stones and even scratched by squealing squaws who swooped down upon us like flies descending on a molasses barrel.

I saw one toothless squaw seize Patricia's braid and give it such a yank that Pat fell out of the saddle. A warrior pushed the squaw away but did not seem interested in stopping the sticks and pebbles. Two of the stones that hit me were big enough to hurt.

But Patricia suffered more from the squaws than I did. Two braves were pushing her toward the biggest lodge, each holding an arm tightly. Another walked ahead—this was the sub-chief. Every now and then he made a half-hearted motion to the squaws to stop. But one Indian woman seized Pat's blouse and ripped it half off her shoulders. Another scratched the exposed flesh. Then a rough shove sent Pat sprawling to the ground inside the lodge.

Three warriors took me and tied me fast to a stripped tree. The bonds cut into my wrists and legs; they just yanked 'em tight with hard jerks.

Then the warriors squatted in a semicircle between me and the lodge where Pat was imprisoned and acted as if waiting for someone. The squaws turned their attention to me when the guard before Pat's prison beat 'em off with guttural protests. One slapped me, another raked my face with her fingernails. They were finally ordered away by the warriors but they stood off and spat at me and the small boys tossed pebbles and sticks and nobody tried to stop 'em.

For a half-hour I suffered; then the squaws lost interest and turned to their kettles.

It was pitch dark when I heard horses approaching. Another group of warriors rode into the village and, from the homage paid him, I gathered that the tall leader was the chief of the entire tribe. He dismounted and approached me with a slow triumphant tread. I noticed that his nose had been broken.

He glared down at me and beat his chest. "Me Icado," he grunted.

My hopes sank. I had been sure all along that these were Icado's warriors, but I had kept hoping against hope that Catamo or another chief friendly with Rich would show up and order us released.

"Icado great chief," he said, throwing up one arm to emphasize his boast. "Icado fight white man. Steal cattle."

And he waved toward the other side of the camp where the squaws were busy slaughtering five steers.

"White man no take Icado's grass," he sneered. His mouth curled in a cruel smile. "Icado take white squaw to his lodge," he added. "Icado have white boy help women around camp. White man help women."

And with that he turned to three of his warriors and ordered my release. He chattered to them in the Arapaho tongue and their faces split into grins as he talked. Then I was pushed toward the carcasses of the slaughtered cows. A skinning knife was thrust into my hand and I was told, with insulting gestures, to start dressing the animals. When I hesitated, three squaws leaped upon me with squeals of delight and raked my face and shoulders with their fingernails. Another beat on me with a heavy stick.

No doubt of it, they would have beaten me to death then and there. I went to work with the skinning knife. The slaughtered cow carried our trail brand. It was a two-year-old we had bought from Magruder.

The squaws stopped work to gloat over me. Actually this was nothing new to me; I had butchered beeves before. But an Indian scorned such menial work and it tickled the Arapahos to watch a white man being bossed around by Indian squaws. The warriors now sat around a campfire, the late arrivals eating out of the same steaming kettle. When I dared look around at them I saw that they had a jug of whiskey and were sampling it freely.

I worked submissively, starting on another carcass as soon I had completed that one. The warriors still drank around their campfire but the squaws, except for those helping me, had been ordered off to the lodges and tepees. Now it was quiet. I was glad of that. The babble had been enough to drive a man loco.

They did not sing or dance as I had expected Indians would; they drank and talked, with Icado doing most of the speechmaking. The others sat on their haunches and watched him as he paced around the fire, throwing his arms above his head, obviously promising them further triumphs over the hated white man. I could not understand a word he said, of course, but several times he pointed to the lodge where Patricia was being held a prisoner.

I bent my head over the bleeding steer. I had to get away. I had studied the terrain as we had been driven into the village; I was sure I could locate Rich's camp from here. I could get to the camp by daylight, I mused. Then we could be back in two hours with a crew of hard-riding, hard-fighting men and take this village apart.

The three squaws were older women, one of them a toothless hag. They had finally stopped pestering me and one even helped me roll over a carcass. They were doing, I noticed, a pretty good job of skinning the steers. One was scraping the inside of a hide with her knife while another was chopping up cuts of meat.

I took a deep breath, then leaped for the brush. I thought surely my bolt would take them by surprise.

But one of the damned squaws seemed to sense my purpose. She dived in front of me and I tripped over her. I scrambled to my feet and kicked off her clutching hands. But another bore down on me brandishing her knife. I turned on her but too late. The knife buried itself in my shoulder and the camp and the squealing woman and the black night swam before my eyes until, finally, all was one.

# CHAPTER ELEVEN

I could not have been unconscious long, for when I came to the fire was still burning and the Indians still listening to Icado. They had carried me back to the stripped tree but this time they had bound me carelessly. I could work my hands a little but when I tried pressing against the bonds my shoulder ached like so many red-hot irons were biting into it. I had a fever and my throat was parched. But I also knew it would be a waste of effort to call out for water.

My head cleared some. I lay very still, fighting off the urge to sleep. I couldn't sleep. I had to wait 'til they had talked themselves out, then work free of the rawhide and get to Rich's camp someway or somehow.

I heard approaching horses. More Indians, I thought, with probably another stealing to brag about. The warriors leaped up, their weapons in hand, but the voice calling out of the dark was evidently known to them, for the red men sat down again, all but Icado. Then into the firelight rode Tim and Jeb Mulloy and dismounted. Tim shook hands with the Arapaho chieftain.

I tried to listen to their talk, rolling over slightly so I could watch them, but their voices were too slow. I could see Icado pointing to the lodge in which my sister was held, then to me. And Tim Mulloy came stalking over to see for himself. I lay still my eyes closed while he bent over me. His cousin, Jeb, was right behind.

"It's the Haines button!" Tim exclaimed.

"Sure as shooting," Jeb said behind him. "And the gal they got must be his sister."

Tim turned me over gently. "Hurt pretty bad," he murmured. He lit a match and pulled back my shirt and looked at my wound. I lay there limp as if I didn't know what was going on.

"Jeb, bandage up this hole," he told his cousin. "This button will bleed to death unless something is done for him."

"What in the hell have I got to make a bandage with?" growled Jeb.

"Use his shirt," Tim said. Jeb was a little rough with his motions. I moaned. Then I croaked:

"Water, water."

"Get him some water first," Tim told Jeb.

"Where?"

"At the creek."

"Hell's bells," growled Jeb, "I didn't sign on to be a nursemaid to a damned Haines."

But he went for the water, bringing it back in his hat. He jerked my head up and poured the liquid down my throat. He wasn't gentle but at least I got a drink. Then Jeb tore the tail off my shirt and bandaged the hole.

I flopped back as soon as he freed me.

Jeb rejoined his cousin and Icado at the fire.

I could make a little out of their palaver. There was something about a thousand dollars. Icado was talking in broken English and I couldn't understand him and Tim's voice was too low.

Then suddenly I heard Tim say to Jeb: "Let's take 'em and get out of here, Jeb. He might change his mind."

"What do you want to buy 'em for?" Jeb protested as they walked toward me. "You're the dangest guy I ever saw. First you don't want to harm 'em. Then you buy 'em from a stinking redskin for a thousand dollars."

"Two reasons, Jeb," grated Tim. "You're too dumb to figger out either."

"What are they?"

"First, I don't want 'em to get hurt. That Icado was aiming to make the girl his wife and I'm not standing for that. Second, I got 'em. I'll keep 'em . . . until Frank Haines comes after 'em."

Jeb sucked in his breath.

"Will he fall for that?"

"Hell, yes," Tim said impatiently. "Any man would."

He bent over me. "Jeb, you bandage a wound like I'd shear a sheep," he grunted.

He fumbled with the crude dressing. Then he took his own kerchief and tightened the packed cloth over the hole. I was in no shape to fight him though I felt like it. Which was worse, to be an

Indian captive or to be handed over to a Mulloy as bait?

It hurt me when he lifted me up, though he tried his level best to be gentle. He carried me in his arms. Jeb went for Pat. I heard her scream and knew he wasn't being gentle with her. Tim laid me across the saddle of my own horse and tied me loosely. I opened my eyes cautiously. Pat sat stiffly in her saddle with her hands tied behind her.

"She can't do much riding like that, Tim," Jeb observed.

"We're not going far," Tim said. "Lead her horse, Jeb."

We went at a walk but, even so, I felt my wound starting to bleed again. I began to groan. Jeb cursed me.

"The kid is gonna go, Tim," he said. "What's the use of fooling with him?"

Tim felt of my wound and realized it was bleeding again. He untied me, caught me as I started to roll off, then swung up into his saddle with me, holding me easy in front of him.

"Now that's plumb sweet," jeered Jeb.

"Shut up," Tim snapped.

The gentle rocking of the horse underneath and my fever got the best of me. I went to sleep there in the arms of Tim Mulloy, the man who hated the Haines so bitterly.

I slept only a minute or so; I was awake when

Tim climbed stiffly out of the saddle with me.

"Build a fire, Jeb," he told his cousin.

I opened my eyes and saw that we were standing before the mouth of a cave half way up a timbered bluff. I could hear gurgling water; a spring must be nearby.

Tim carried me into the cave and laid me on the sandy floor. Then I heard him ordering Patricia out of the saddle. She came and lay by me, her hands still bound.

"Are you all right, Pete?" she asked anxiously.

"*Bueno*," I whispered.

"Cut these bonds and let me tend to my brother," Pat begged Tim Mulloy.

He freed her hands without a reply. Now the fire threw a faint shimmering light over the mouth of the cave.

"Jeb will put coffee on to boil," Tim told my sister. "There is some grub piled up back there. Scurry around and see if you can fix up anything for your brother."

Pat covered me with blankets that smelled of perspiration and horse flesh but at least were warm. She placed another under my head as a high pillow, halfway propping me up. Then I heard her say to Jeb:

"Will you get me some water, please?"

"Hell, I ain't no nursemaid," he answered.

"Get her the water, Jeb," Tim Mulloy snapped.

"Don't be so danged free with your orders,

Tim," the cousin shot back. "I ain't no peon."

"I'll get it," Pat said. There was a helplessness in her tone, and yet a determination.

"Empty out them coffee grounds," Tim suggested, "and boil water in that."

In a few moments she had my shirt open and was bathing the wound with hot water. It bled a little again, but she stopped that with a fresh bandage.

I lay there unable to open my eyes, it seemed, but still able to hear every word. I heard Tim ask:

"Will he be all right?"

"I don't know," Pat answered. "He has a high fever and he has bled a lot."

"There's plenty of whiskey," Tim pointed out.

"I don't want to give him whiskey until his fever runs down," my sister said.

"Well, I ain't got a fever," Jeb Mulloy chuckled. "Me for the whiskey."

Pat fed me a thin soup made out of canned tomatoes and potatoes. I gulped it eagerly, though it seemed tasteless to me. I couldn't get enough of anything to drink. I was sleepy and wanted to drop off but my thirst kept me awake. Pat gave me drink after drink.

Through a fog I heard her plead with Tim Mulloy.

"Mr. Mulloy, my brother will die unless I can get him to a doctor. Please let us go."

"No," he said firmly. But he bent over me and felt of my face.

"Keep his wound clean and keep feeding him liquids," he told her. "That fever of his is only natural. If it ain't dropped by morning, I'll bring a doctor out here. That's all I can do."

Pat sobbed. "If he dies, I'll . . . I'll . . ."

"I ain't gonna let him die, gal," Tim assured her roughly.

"What are you keeping us here for? If you want to kill us because we are Frank Haines' children, go ahead and get it over with."

"I'm not going to kill you. I'm not going to hurt you."

"What do you want with us then?"

"Your dad will come looking for you," he explained grimly. "I want to see your dad."

"You'll . . . murder him . . . won't you!"

"I want to fight him," Tim said doggedly. "I'll give him a show. My kid didn't have that."

He turned off. Then dead sleep struck me between the eyes.

A lot of time passed . . . one day, maybe two. I didn't know for sure. I don't think I was ever delirious but most of the time I lay there in a dull stupor, unable to even raise my head or even turn over. I felt Pat by me nearly all the time; she poured water down my parched throat and made me drink the soups she concocted out of the meagre store of food supplies. Then the fever left me all of a sudden and the shoulder felt better. I was lying there able to hear, even to talk, but without the strength to raise up.

It was like waking from a long sleep. I whispered to Pat and her face lit up with joy. She hugged me.

"He's better!" she cried to Jeb.

He walked over and regarded me with a scowl. "Thought you were gonna kick the bucket," he said, then turned on his heel and strode out of the cave.

"Anything . . . about . . . Dad?" I asked painfully.

"Don't worry about anything," Pat ordered me. "You lie there still and get well."

She fed me again, with sourdough biscuits in the soup this time. She had just finished when we heard a horse outside. It was Tim Mulloy riding back. He looked tired. Deep lines were etched in his lean dark face. He sprawled out on the sandy floor of the cave and reached for the whiskey jug.

"Fix me some grub, Jeb," he sighed. "I'm tuckered."

"Cook it yourself," was the surly answer.

Tim Mulloy scowled at his cousin. "You've been hitting this whiskey, haven't you?"

"Why not?" was Jeb's defiant retort. "Sittin' around here, cooped up in this cave . . . gotta do something to pass the time."

Tim turned to my sister. "How's the boy?"

"Better," she answered. "He was conscious a little while ago."

Tim came to my pallet and bent over me. I had closed my eyes and I pretended to be asleep.

"Seems better to me," he said. "Fever has gone down."

He walked back to the mouth of the cave, sat down and reached for the jug again. He took a deep drink, then rolled a smoke. He continued to eye his cousin.

"Jeb," he said slowly. "I've been thinking about you and the gal here. If you get likkered up and harm her, I'll kill you with my own hands."

"I ain't bothering the gal," Jeb growled.

"You ain't smart any time," Tim rasped, "but you're hawg wild when you've had a few snorts. I got you out of that scrape in Encinal, but not anymore. This one I'll handle myself."

"Ask her," grunted Jeb. "I ain't laid a hand on her."

Tim turned to Patricia.

"No," she nodded, "he hasn't."

"See that you keep it up," Tim said crisply. He added in a moment: "When I ride back in, I'll carry what's left of this jug with me. I'm afraid to trust you, Jeb. You may mean well this time but you can't hold your likker. A few drinks and you act like a plumb damned fool."

"Some day, Tim," threatened Jeb, "you're gonna ride me too much."

"Shut up," snapped the older Mulloy. "You'll never have the nerve to draw on me and you know it."

Tim cooked bacon and beans for himself. He ate hurriedly and without further talk. He left as soon as he had finished, without washing his plate or cup, and he took the jug with him as he had threatened.

Jeb chuckled as his cousin disappeared. "I got another hid," he told Patricia. And he produced a jug from the rear of the cave. He jerked out the stopper and raised it to his lips. "Tim ain't near as smart as he thinks," he confided to Pat.

"You certainly let him kick you around," she said coldly.

"I can stop that any time I want to," Jeb boasted, fired up by her remark. "I could spot him the draw and still shoot his guts out."

Pat left her seat at the mouth of the cave. She came back to my pallet, bathed my face with fresh water, gave me a drink, straightened the pillow under my head.

"I'm going to try something, Pete," she whispered.

Then she returned to the dying fire.

"What do you let him treat you like that for?" she demanded. "I don't see how a man can stand it."

"I ain't such a fool," said Jeb. "Tim has a big

spread and money in the bank. I'm the only Mulloy left. I'll put up with him."

"For the rest of his life?" asked Pat. "That's a long time to be treated like a hound pup."

Jeb took another deep drink. There was a long silence. Then he said slowly, with a sort of whine in his voice.

"Things can happen." He wagged his shaggy head. "Things can happen," he repeated.

I fell off to sleep again. The morning sun slanting into the cave woke me, and for the first time I felt like raising up on my elbows and looking around. Jeb was snoring on his blanket, lying flat on his back with one hand resting on the jug.

"He drank himself out," Pat said in disgust.

"No sign of Dad?"

"No." She thought a moment. "I don't think he'll come, Pete. I believe he is smart enough to scent a trap."

"If he'd go to Rich, then . . ."

"He won't do that," she said firmly. "I don't want him to. You know Rich's way. He'd ride right up to the cave and . . ."

"Shoot the daylights outa Jeb and Tim," I finished. "That's his way all right. And I'd sure like to see him come storming up that ridge."

Now Jeb stirred. He raised up, then fell back with a groan. He lay there as if in torment.

Pat had kindled the fire and was cooking

breakfast. She cut more bacon and put the coffeepot on. She brought me a tin plate, then filled one for Jeb.

"Here, Jeb," she said. Hers wasn't an unkind tone; nobody could help feeling sorry for Jeb.

He raised up, blinked, took a bite of bacon, then pushed it away.

"I can't eat," he moaned. "I can't eat a bite."

His eyes were bloodshot. Seeing the jug, he reached for it with a trembling hand.

"Need an eye-opener," he mumbled.

He took a swig, then lowered the jug with what was at once a moan and a sigh. The whiskey had a quick effect on him. His eyes lost their glazed look. Pat motioned to his plate but he did not want food.

"Gotta drink myself out of this," he grinned. So quickly had he revived.

Pat fed me. Jeb watched for a moment, then gestured to the coffee boiling on the fire.

"Think I could stand a shot of that," he hinted.

Pat poured him a cupful. "No sugar," he said. "Black. Black and strong."

He tried to hold the cup but it shook, splashing hot liquid over his hand. He swore mildly. "Too danged hot." In a moment he gulped down half the contents."

"Now," he sighed, "that makes a man feel better."

His eyes were still bloodshot but they were

almost friendly as they followed Pat's motions as she fed me. I was hungry this time; I ate beans and bacon and biscuits.

"That button," observed Jeb, "is gonna live. No dying man ever put away a meal like that."

He was turning to the jug again, taking small drinks.

"He's much better," Pat agreed.

Jeb drained the rest of the coffee. "You ain't such bad people," he reflected. "I'll be damned if you ain't nicer to me than my own kin."

He took another drink. His head rolled from side to side. Quickly he had reached that stage of drunkenness when he was mulling over his own misfortunes.

"You'd think," he sighed, "that with just me and Tim left he'd treat me whiter. I done some things for that hombre, too. I slapped his brand on a hundred mavericks anyhow last winter. But I'm just a hired hand to him, a guy to kick around."

Pat refilled his coffee for him.

"Why don't you come out and say it?" she demanded, sitting by him at the fire. "Why don't you come right out and own up that you hate your cousin?"

Jeb studied her a moment without a muscle in his face stirring. Then his lips parted in a snarl.

"I ain't denying it," he said. "Sure I hate his guts. I got a right to."

"Sure you do," agreed Pat. "Lemme see your gun."

He slapped her hand away as she reached for it. "Don't try to pull anything on me," he snapped.

"I want to count the notches, that's all," she explained. "You've killed men, haven't you?"

"Some," he admitted cautiously.

"I heard talk down in the Frio," went on my sister. "They said you used to be a gun slick."

"Some," he conceded again, still suspicious.

"That's why Tim keeps you, isn't it? Don't he pack you around with him so you can shoot the two of you outa trouble?"

Jeb chuckled. "Don't reckon Tim could do much on his own," he said. "Take your dad now. If your dad would take his gun and work on it, he'd be able to beat Tim in a month's time. Tim's a trigger squeezer. Got a heavy finger."

"Why don't you work for people who would pay you more money?" Pat demanded.

The jug rolled over and a few drops gurgled out before Pat retrieved it.

"What do you mean?"

"Some people pay good money for gun slicks," Pat told him. "A hundred a month and up. A man who isn't afraid and who is good with a gun doesn't have to be treated like an ordinary hand and booted around by a no-good cuss like Tim Mulloy."

"I told you before," he answered. There was that sort of whining apology in his tone again. "I'm Tim's last kin. If I stick with him, I'll get his spread."

"When he dies," nodded Pat. She smiled, a fierce smile. "Or when he is killed."

Jeb started. He stared at her from under his bushy brows.

"Yeah," he muttered. "Or when he is killed."

He took a bigger drink than usual. He lay back against the side of the cave.

"I've thought about that some," he admitted. "I ain't ashamed of it. I don't wanna do it. But some day when he's kicking me around and talking so uppity . . ."

"I'm getting to that," Pat said a little impatiently. "My father ought to kill Tim himself. Or hire it done."

Jeb nodded. For the moment the inflection in her words was lost upon him.

"Could hire it done easy," he admitted. His lips parted in an unpleasant grin. "Can't say as I'd be too mad at the waddy who did it either," he mumbled.

"Of course you wouldn't," Pat cried. "For the man who killed Tim Mulloy would be doing us and you both a favor. They'd be giving us both a jump. We'd be free of him and you'd be better off for your own spread."

He stared at her. "I'd get it," he said slowly, as

if convincing himself. "I'd get it even without his say so."

"Sure you would. You're his last living relative, aren't you?"

Jeb's eyes were gleaming. He rocked back and forth a moment. Then he reached for the jug again.

"Get your dad to hire 'em a fighting man," he said after a moment. "Tell him to bushwhack Tim . . . anything. I'll sit it out."

Pat came back to my pallet in answer to my call for a drink of water.

"We can do it," I whispered to her excitedly. "We've got some money. We can hire a killer in this Indian Territory and when Tim gets his . . ."

"I know it," she nodded. She bent over and kissed me lightly on the cheek. There was a smile on her lips, a faint one. But there was a gleam in her eye that showed she meant business.

Jeb was talking thicker now. "Get a man to do it," he grated. "Tim Mulloy has it coming to him even if he is my own cousin. He'd be a sucker for a good fighting man. Why, I could take . . ."

"Why don't you?" Pat proposed crisply. "Why don't you do it yourself, Jeb Mulloy?"

"Me!" he gasped.

"Sure. You're the one he has kicked around. You oughta wanna to get even with him on your own. And we'll pay you, Jeb Mulloy. We'll pay you in cash."

He studied her with a hollow look.

"T'ain't right," he answered after a moment. "No matter how he treats me, he's my last kin. Though it's true that . . ."

His voice fell off.

"What is true?" Pat demanded.

Jeb shook his head. "Done talked too much already," he muttered.

Pat leaned over him. "Would you kill him for six thousand dollars?" she asked. "For six thousand in gold?"

"You got six thousand?"

"In our saddlebags," my sister nodded.

Jeb rolled to his feet. He walked out of the cave, staggering from the whiskey he had gulped. He rolled back in a moment later.

"You ain't lying," he said. "You got the six thousand?"

"Sure," Pat said fiercely. "Do you want it, Jeb Mulloy?"

"Yep," he nodded. "I reckon I do."

He jerked up the jug and took a heavy drink. He turned back to Pat with his eyes gleaming and his lips parted in a coarse grin.

"I thought some out there," he told her, jerking his thumb toward the mouth of the cave. "You're right, girlie. I'm Jeb Mulloy and nobody has any right to kick me around. Nobody ever did except my own cousin. I'm fast with a gun and I'm taking charge of this spread right now."

"Good!" Pat cried.

He took a step toward her, that grin still on his unshaven lips.

"I ain't listening to a thing Tim says," he snarled. "I'm gonna shoot him down like he was nothing but a cottontail rabbit. Who in the hell is he to boss me around?"

He rolled back and forth on his feet a moment. Then he reached out suddenly and caught Pat's shoulder.

"Come here," he grunted. "Come here and gimme a kiss."

"No," she refused. She laughed but not mirthfully. She was trying to talk him out of this sudden mood.

But there was no moving him. "Ain't no use to fight back," he gloated over her. "I'm gonna have my way around here."

His weight bore her down to her knees. "Please, Jeb!" she begged, and there was fear in her voice now.

I raised up. My left side was a blaze of pain but I gritted my teeth against it. Jeb had torn her blouse from her shoulder. In a moment he would have her subdued.

A rifle, Jeb's gun, lay a dozen feet from my pallet. I crawled toward it. He was too busy wrestling with Pat to pay me any heed.

Then, above their scuffling, above Jeb's grunting, above Patricia's whimpering, I heard a horse coming up the trail.

Then Tim Mulloy stepped into the cave.

He seemed startled for a moment, then he leaped forward and caught Jeb's shoulder and spun him around. He slapped his cousin roughly and pushed him away, sent him sprawling.

"Damn you, Jeb, you're through," Tim snarled. "I'm washing my hands of you."

Patricia stood up, pulling her torn blouse over her shoulder. Jeb also climbed to his feet. He looked at Tim with eyes that blazed his hatred.

"I mean it," Tim repeated. He tossed a handful of bills to the sandy floor.

"That's all you'll ever get out of me. Pull out."

Tim turned his back on his cousin with that and asked me how I felt. Before I could answer Jeb's voice roared out:

"Turn around, Tim. I don't wanna shoot you in the back."

Tim turned. Jeb was crouching there, one hand almost touching his gun. His intent was unmistakable.

"Don't be a fool, Jeb," Tim said. I'm not sure, but I think his voice shook a little.

"I've been a long time getting around to this," Jeb gloated. The fear he usually showed for his cousin was gone. It had always been, I suppose, a mental awe rather than a physical fear. Certainly Jeb Mulloy, a big man and one who had used his guns before, had no reason to be afraid of anyone physically.

"Put that gun down, Jeb," Tim snapped.

But it didn't work. This time Jeb Mulloy wasn't taking orders.

"You don't wanna fight me, do you, Tim?" Jeb sneered. "You know I'm a better man than you are, don't you? I'll give you a little time, Tim. Then if you ain't got the guts to draw, I'll drill you anyhow."

"Jeb, don't make me . . ."

"Shut up," roared Jeb. "From now I'm doing the talking. You're listening, Tim Mulloy."

He came a half-step closer. "I've been working up to this," he said hoarsely. "You kicked me about because I was a poor cousin. You ordered me around like I was a peon. My pap never had a ranch like yours. You were the rich man handing out your lousy charity to your cousins. Well, think about that ranch of yours, Tim. I'm gonna take it. I'm gonna take it lock, stock and barrel."

"Jeb, don't go off half-cocked," protested Tim. "Maybe I spoke too quick. But . . ."

"There ain't no buts, Tim," growled Jeb. "I've been looking forward to this. It ain't no new notion of mine. I knew the day I rode up to your spread that I was gonna beat you out of it. I took it easy 'cause I was in no hurry. But I got rid of the kid . . ."

"You what!" snapped Tim Mulloy.

"Sure," Jeb gloated. "You thought Frank

Haines did it, didn't you? I dropped him, Tim. I dropped him because he hated me and he threatened me. Told me he'd have you run me off. I get your ranch when you're gone. Think of that."

"Jeb, you bastard!" growled Tim. "Did you kill Skippy? Answer me!"

"Sure I dropped him," said Jeb with an evil chuckle. "Dropped him right between the shoulder blades. He caught me slipping a gold-piece out of your pocketbook. He was gonna tell you. He didn't like me. He treated me like dirt like you did."

Tim Mulloy came forward a pace. His lean face was black in his rage.

"Makes you riled, doesn't it, Tim," sneered Jeb. "Are you riled enough to make a fight of it. Go for your gun when you're ready."

Tim stopped, still holding Jeb with his intent stare. He made no motion toward his holster. He was, I thought, weighing his chances. They were small.

Jeb laughed . . . a laugh that made me shudder.

Then as I turned away I saw a sight that made me go as stiff as a poker!

Around the mouth of the cave, weight almost flat against the sides, my father came slipping!

He was more like a scarecrow than a man but I knew him at once. He had not shaved in many a day, nor had his hair cut, and his clothes hung in tatters from a body that had shed at least thirty pounds. He lifted a hand in silent warning as he noticed my stare.

Jeb's back was toward him and Jeb was unmistakably the target of his stealthy advance.

I started again. Right behind Dad, moving as cautiously, came Martin Champion.

Tim Mulloy saw them but did not give it away by either gesture or expression. Instead he played for time.

"Can't we make a deal, Jeb?" he whined. He was, I thought, stalling until my father got close enough to grab Jeb from behind. "I'll make you a partner. I'll help you start your own herd."

Dad came another long silent step.

"I didn't get to see Skippy kick," Jeb said cruelly. "But I'll see your death kicking, Tim. I'll stick around for it."

Now Dad was no more than six feet from Jeb. Champion and he launched ready to spring. Then . . .

A twig snapped under one of them. Jeb Mulloy whirled.

I heard Jeb's curse, then his quick shot. Dad had leaped but Jeb's draw was fast. Dad spun around and landed on his face. Jeb pumped a shot at Champion and the newspaper publisher fell backward.

Then Tim Mulloy's gun blazed out. The cave shook from the explosions. Smoke drifted up and around. I heard Patricia scream and I tried to squirm toward Dad.

Jeb Mulloy was still on his feet and he was pumping his trigger. But he was shooting wild. One bullet tore through my blanket.

Then Jeb toppled forward. Tim Mulloy stood over him grimly for a moment, then replaced his gun in its holster.

Pat was ripping away Dad's shirt. Tim watched her a moment, then bent over and gave his attention to Champion.

Tim spoke first.

"This one is just winged," he said in a dull voice. "Hole in the shoulder, that's all."

Pat didn't answer. She tore at her petticoat and frantically tried to stop the flow of blood from Dad's chest. I rolled over to him in spite of the pain.

He lay looking at us with that gleam in his eyes that always set me a-quiver. He reached out for me with a shaky hand.

"Howdy, Pete," he murmured.

"Got this one up," Tim said brusquely. "Can I help you, Miss?"

"I don't think so," Pat whispered. "I don't think . . . anyone can."

Tim stood over the three of us. Dad met his look squarely.

"A damned shame, Haines," Tim said through tight lips. "A damned shame."

"Sure, Tim," Dad murmured. "A damned shame."

"Never like to hate a man, Tim," he said faintly. Obviously every word was a strain. "Let's shake and get it over with."

Tim Mulloy bent his head. He had not taken Dad's hand.

"No," he said after a moment. "No," he added harshly. "I ain't got that coming, Haines. Not now. But if I live long enough and . . ."

He turned suddenly and stalked out of the cave.

Dad put the hand Mulloy had refused upon my shoulder. "He'll be a friend from here on, Pete," he whispered. "The best kind."

His eyes closed. His lips were still working but it was hard to hear what he was saying. I leaned close.

"So is Champion, Pete," he added. "So is Rich. Can't change the draw, Pete. Play 'em like they are."

Then he called out: "Pat, Pat! Where are you?"

"Here, Dad," my sister gulped.

"Here," he murmured, reaching for her. "Put your cheek . . . close to mine . . . like you did when you were a little girl—"

She obeyed him. Then his hand tightened on my shoulder. It was my wounded shoulder and the pressure of his fingers was almost more than I could stand. But I didn't move his hand.

"So long, Pete," he whispered. "So long, Pat. Wish the three of us could . . ."

There was no quiver of his body. The only thing that happened was that all of a sudden he wasn't living any more. His hand dropped from my shoulder, I guess with just about the last spark of life he had left.

We lay there a long time without making a sound, Pat and me and the dead man we had loved. Then somebody said:

"Dead?"

I looked around. Martin Champion was sitting up.

"Yes," Pat nodded.

"I'm sorry," he said slowly.

He sighed. "I guess," he declared unhappily, "I made a mess of things, Pat. Maybe it would have been better if you and I had stayed out of it and Pete and his compadre, Rich Stewart, had handled it their way."

"No," my sister said firmly. She stood up. She stood straight and proud.

"Dad didn't want Rich turned loose either," she added.

"Rich would have gotten him first," I snapped. "If we had left it to Rich, Dad wouldn't be here . . . like . . ."

"I know, son, I know," Martin admitted. In a moment he added: "But just killing Tim Mulloy, and maybe Jeb, wasn't the answer, Pete. Your father had to be free of that charge against him."

"How did he get in touch with you?" I demanded. "Why didn't he go to Rich . . . to somebody he could depend on?"

"Pete!" snapped my sister.

"That's all right, Pat," Champion said with a faint smile. "Let him alone."

Then: "He didn't come to me, Pete. I found him."

"Why? What business was it of yours?"

"I made it mine, Pete," he answered mildly. "The minute I talked to Pat . . . and fell in love with her . . . I made it mine."

"In love with her!" I scorned. "And her as good as engaged to . . ."

It was Pat who stopped us. "This talk is doing no good," she said coldly. "We have to get Dad's body into Cimarron."

She did most of it, for Champion and I were near helpless. She rolled Dad's body over and over until she had him outside the cave, then she struggled a moment trying to lift the corpse into the saddle. I gave her a suggestion and she tied a rope around Dad's waist, then made the other end fast to the saddlehorn on my horse. That way the animal did the hoisting.

Then she helped Champion and me onto our horses. By riding sideways I could stand the horse's walk.

It was slow business. The newspaper publisher

and I couldn't get enough water to drink. Once, when we stopped at a water hole, Pat remembered to look in her saddlebags. The six thousand dollars we had left Cimarron with was still there.

"I hope," Pat sighed, "the delay didn't hurt Rich."

"It couldn't be helped," I said. "We did the best we could."

"Yes," she agreed. She looked back at the lifeless man tied across Jeb Mulloy's horse.

"So did he," she said with a catch in her voice.

It was near night when we got to town. I reckon we were about the sorriest bunch of riders ever to come into Cimarron. One of us dead, two of us winged, and only a slim girl to prod us on.

As soon as we had dismounted Pat asked Luke to send for Rich.

He came galloping in next morning. Pat handed him the money.

"We were taking it to you," she explained, "when the Arapahos . . ."

He studied the bag of gold. "Yours?" he guessed.

"Ours," she corrected him.

"I hate to use it," he said slowly. "I'd rather get it some other way."

"What are friends for, Rich?"

She asked it in a soft voice, her gaze meeting his frankly. He looked at her sharply. He had a way of doing that, of slightly tilting his head and regarding something with an intent set look.

"They're to stand with," he answered after a moment. There was a shortness in his voice. "Thanks for the jump," he added.

Then he patted her shoulder. "About Frank," he murmured. "Leave it all to me."

She went hurriedly to her room. She was crying as she started up the steps and she was stumbling blindly before she reached the top.

Rich turned to me with a sigh. "I'll get you up to bed, pardner," he said. "And Luke here is a good sawbones in a pinch."

I let him help me up the stairs and permitted Luke to undress me.

"How are things going?" I asked Rich. "Did you get the boys—Black John and them—to wait?"

"They're sticking," he nodded.

Then, flapping his hand against his thigh: "The General is getting more complaints. There will be another hearing. Unless I've got the goods on this whiskey running pronto, I'll lose out."

I sighed. Everything seemed to be going against us.

"But we can't worry about that now," Rich went on. "Right now we got to have a good funeral for Frank Haines."

And it was a good funeral. Dad wouldn't have liked it. Pat didn't. At first she held out for a simple ceremony. Then she gave in.

"They want to do something so bad," she explained to me with a wan smile.

Which they did. And making a fuss over it was the only way they knew to show how they felt. There were Rich and all of his riders, and Lula Belle and her saloon crowd, and a group of Indians including Catamo himself, and the boys from Magruder's trail herd which had just stormed in.

And there were plenty of the homesteaders who had, in my books, no right to come.

Rich ran things. That was his way. But it was Martin Champion who spoke just before the board casket was lowered into the grave.

I was with Rich when he asked the newspaper man to make the talk. "You shine with your gab," he said. "Could you read the rites for Frank Haines?"

I was a little surprised at Rich's choice. It was usual for Rich to divide things. A man stood one way or he stood another.

"It would be a privilege," Martin Champion answered quickly.

For Pat's sake I was glad Rich had asked him.

He could talk, that man. He stood there with bowed head and the words rolled from his lips.

"Heavenly Father, in Thy infinite wisdom Thou has seen fit to take Frank Haines unto your bosom and to breathe into his soul the glories of everlasting life . . ."

I raised my head once and looked around. Patricia was sobbing; she leaned against me for support. Coming up slowly, in twos and threes, some of them in their everyday clothes, the homesteaders listened reverently. Catamo and the Arapahos did not bow their heads, probably the Indians were mentally speculating upon the queer notions of the white man. They seemed actually sad that a great warrior had gone to the Happy Hunting Grounds. Lula Belle and her girls and her bartenders and her gamblers stood away from the rest of us. Most of them cried, too. Champion could do that with words.

Then it was over and we went slowly back to the hotel. Patricia retired to her room again.

"Come stay with me, Pete," she begged.

I couldn't refuse. We sat in her room and watched the sun go down. For an hour I know not a word passed between us. Then I said:

"That Champion, he can make a speech."

"It was the most beautiful thing I ever heard," Patricia murmured.

Then she added, as an afterthought: "His man got elected, Pete."

"President?"

"Yes. Grover Cleveland."

She didn't want to go down for supper and Luke set us a table in her room. Then Pat pleaded a headache and went to bed with the chickens.

I went down into the lobby. Rich had ridden

back to his camp right after the funeral. Lula Belle's was closed out of respect for my father.

I walked up and down the street once. Dennis Cameron nodded to me as I passed him.

Then I heard a small voice say, "Mister Haines."

The nester girl who had egged on my licking at the hands of the homesteader was standing there twisting her hands shyly.

"What is it?" I snapped.

"I just wanted to tell you," she mumbled, "that I'm sorry . . . about your dad."

"Thanks," I said gruffly, too much so, and walked on.

# CHAPTER TWELVE

The next day Champion explained to me the part he had played in my father's hiding.

"I talked to Pat and then to you," the publisher said awkwardly, "and I knew your father couldn't have shot down a boy in cold blood. It was by luck, pure luck, that I was able to contact Frank Haines, and persuade him to trust me. We liked each other at once, Pete."

I remembered the note left for us at the hotel. Yes, Champion admitted, he had written it.

"I wanted to do two things," he went on. "I wanted to hire a detective to investigate the case. His report was favorable. I have it in my safe if you ever want to look at it, though there is little need of it now. There was no material evidence that your father killed Skippy Mulloy. I was ready to propose that your father return to Texas for trial when this came up. Perhaps he would have been convicted by a local jury. But then we would have appealed the case and had the verdict set aside. If not that, I could get a pardon for him. I was reasonably sure of that. I had written a brief and a friend of mine had presented it to the Governor of Texas. . . ."

I blinked. "You got friends that can ask favors like that of the Governor?" I demanded, finding it a little hard to believe him.

He nodded. "My father has influence," he admitted. "I have some in my own right. The incoming Governor of Texas is a friend of my family's. However, Pete, that only meant he would review the case. He studied it, and found nothing to support Mulloy's charge, and the warrant issued for your father's arrest, except the feud between the two men. That isn't sufficient in any court of law to convict any man . . . in any unbiased court, that is."

I didn't answer. Martin studied me. "I did my best, Pete," he said mildly. "I hope you no longer resent my interference."

"I got no grudge," I said, too crisply I'm sure. "I just don't like your way of coming out of the chute, Champion. I cotton to Rich Stewart's style."

"I know that," he nodded. He stared at the floor a minute, then raised his eyes. "I hope," he said gently, "you change your mind about that, Pete. A man can't ride hell-for-leather through life shooting it out with anybody who crosses him."

"I like his style," I repeated stubbornly.

"I can understand that," he agreed. "I admire it also, Pete, believe it or not. There was another breed of men like him once, a long time ago. They wore suits of chain mail and carried long lances and . . ."

He stopped with a short laugh. "And one of them," he added, "fought a windmill."

• • •

The days dragged until I was able to ride again. By then the first northers had blown in and on south. Winter had come to the Cimarron. There was a haze in the sky of a morning, and the stem grass was blue-green no longer, but corn yellow.

It seemed like time galloped on, because, I guess, I was so busy. We had finally talked some of the hoemen into cutting grass for us. They had bedded down for the winter across the river, most of 'em, building dugouts and using their credit at Nathan Stool's. A church was built and there were two more stores and the town was getting right pert-like.

But not again did Champion challenge our cattle company in his paper. We were getting along *bueno* except for the unceasing Indian forays. Rich put on four more riders and his men patrolled the fences, always on guard. They shot off one raid and I rode out and made a full report and sent it in to General Sheridan's headquarters. Icado bothered some of the outlying settlements but the *Bugle* made only casual mention of this.

"What's the trouble?" I asked Champion one night. "You seem to be trying to get along with us lately."

Which was true. The whole town was getting plumb friendly. Champion's paper ran advertisements and local notices and long-winded editorials about what the new president, Grover

Cleveland, would do as soon as he took office.

He and Patricia were spending more and more time with each other. They read the same books and when the doctor's wife brought in a piano Pat took lessons from her and a group of them listened to music and sang at the physician's house one or two evenings a week.

"I would say, Pete," Martin smiled, "that I am adopting a new strategy."

"You're playing with fire if you don't know it," I told him coldly. "This stirring up trouble among the Indians is going to mean trouble for somebody."

"It should," he nodded. "I can't understand why General Sheridan hasn't intervened before."

"I can tell you," I snapped. "The General has a notion who is behind this whiskey running."

"I know," Champion said slowly. "Stewart charges that Purdy and Mulloy are a combine against him, and that I'm aiding them."

"Aren't you?"

"We are not giving whiskey to the Indians," he answered firmly. "They are taking the cash Stewart pays them and buying it themselves."

"Icado is the one causing the trouble and you know it," I said hotly.

"Pete," smiled Champion, "let's declare an armistice. I can readily understand your devotion to Rich Stewart. But don't be narrow-minded enough to believe that everybody in the world who doesn't think like Rich does is dead wrong."

I refused the olive branch. "When we prove that your compadres are starting this trouble," I growled, "you'll wish you had stayed in Virginia."

Then I wheeled away, fearing I had talked too much. I shouldn't tip them off, I thought, that Rich had men trailing the Purdy riders.

Tim Mulloy had been in town twice. Both times he had bought a single drink at Lula Belle's, then had ridden off. I heard saloon gossip that he was trying to sell out the interests he had hurriedly acquired, the partnership with Purdy. Talk was that Purdy would take over on his own as soon as he acquired the cash to pay Mulloy off.

It was a cool gray December day when Pecos Sherrill rode in for me.

"Rich wants you at the camp pronto," Sherrill said with a grin. "I'll buy a drink, then we'll head right out."

"What's up?" I demanded.

"We picked up a waddy riding through our country," he said. "Was moseying toward the Arapaho camp. Loaded down, too."

"Whiskey!" I exclaimed.

Pecos nodded. "Finally got one of 'em with the goods," he beamed.

"Has he talked?"

"Some," Pecos admitted carefully. His lips twitched. "Contrary cuss," he murmured. "All he wanted to do was stare at us and shake his head."

We hurried to Lula Belle's. I didn't need the drink myself but I knew Pecos wouldn't stir without one. That was a man's right in return for riding into town.

Tim Mulloy was at the bar. I stopped. I wasn't going to drink at the same bar with him.

His glass was half empty. He saw me, turned, bolted down his drink and left the saloon.

I whispered to Lula Belle that Rich had caught a whiskey runner with the goods. Her eyes shone. Her girls had passed on many a tip they had picked up from Purdy's men. But, until now, we hadn't been able to catch anyone with the goods.

"We'll bust this wide open," she said fiercely.

It was late at night when Pecos and I reached Rich's camp. I found the prisoner to be a furtive-eyed sallow-faced man I had seen several times around Cimarron. He was Purdy's man.

Rich was smoking a cigarette and drinking black coffee. There were lines in his face as if he had lost plenty of sleep.

"This hombre," he said, jerking his thumb at the prisoner, "has some talking to do. Get your pencil and paper, Pete, and fix it up right. Then he'll sign it."

I looked to the sallow-faced man for verification. He nodded sullenly.

I chuckled. I didn't need to be told that he had

been a hard one to break down. And I didn't *want* to know the methods employed.

I wrote as rapidly as I could as he told his story, with some prompting by Rich Stewart. He confessed that he had been captured by Rich Stewart and four other Cimarron Cattle Company riders and that on his horse were four gallon jugs of whiskey, one in each saddlebag and two slung across the saddlehorn.

"Where did you get the whiskey?" Rich demanded.

"I done told you," protested the sallow-faced man, who had revealed his identity as Clay Price.

"Tell me again," Rich snapped. "It's got to go into writing."

Price squirmed. "I bought it at Henderson."

"On whose orders?"

"My boss'."

"Who do you work for?"

"The partnership of Bob Purdy and Tim Mulloy."

"Who do you take orders from?"

"Purdy."

"What were you going to do with the whiskey?"

"Was going to deliver it at the Arapaho camp back of the canyon."

"To Icado's tribe?"

"Yes."

"Were those Purdy's orders?"

"Wal," hesitated Price, "it was Purdy who told me to do it this time."

"Have you delivered whiskey to Icado's warriors before?"

"Yes."

"Sometimes by Purdy's orders, sometimes by Mulloy's?"

Price nodded.

"Did you ever deliver ammunition to them, or rifles?" demanded Rich.

"Yes."

"At the orders of Purdy or Mulloy?"

"Yes."

I gestured that I was getting behind. Besides, my fingers were cramped; I needed a rest. Rich poured another cup of coffee and rolled another cigarette and waited grimly. I nodded in a moment for him to proceed.

"Did the Indians ever pay you for the whiskey or the ammunition?"

"No."

"They were gifts?"

"Yes."

"For what?"

Price squirmed. "One time," he said slowly, "I heard 'em talking. They were supplying Icado with whiskey, guns, ammunition and some money and supplies to make trouble for you."

"Who is 'they'?"

"Mulloy, Purdy," shrugged the captive. "And them people in Cimarron."

"What people?"

"That newspaper feller. And the Indian agent, whatever his name is."

"Martin Champion?"

"Yes."

"And Walter Jenson?"

"Yes."

"What did they have to do with it?"

"Oh, I dunno," sighed Price. "They were in cahoots with Tim and Bob. They had a deal on to take your lease away from you and give it back to Purdy."

"Did Champion or Jenson know the Indians were being bribed to make trouble?"

"Jenson did for sure," shrugged Price. Then, in a whining voice: "Ain't that enough? I dunno anything about that inside of the deal. I just ride for Bob. I don't sit in on his palavers."

"I think that's enough," Rich nodded.

He waited until I had finished writing, then motioned to Clay Price.

"Sign it," he ordered.

Price obeyed.

Rich turned to Pecos. "Tie him up and have the boys sit a guard," he said wearily. "We're taking no chances on him getting away."

"Gimme a chance to run for it," begged Price. "You got my story. Lemme get out of the country before Purdy or Mulloy know I've squealed."

Rich shook his head. "You'll face General Sheridan with this," he stated grimly.

"Gawd, no," Price groaned. "They'll get me sure if I do that, Stewart. That ain't no way to treat a man."

"Right now," drawled Rich, "I ain't in such a good humor. I'd kinda like to cut somebody's liver out just for the hell of it."

Price subsided. He submitted peacefully to being bound to a bunk with rawhide strips.

"Now, pardner," Rich said to me, "I'll ride over to Fort Sill and ask General Sheridan to hold another hearing. This time I'll do *all* the talking."

I studied my notes. "We have proof on Mulloy and Purdy," I said. "What about Champion and Jenson? They might wriggle out of it if this is all we have."

"I figger it's enough," he said. "They were hitched up with Purdy."

I remembered Champion's firm denial to me that same day that he and his associates had sent whiskey to the Indians.

"It could be," I murmured, "that Champion doesn't know anything about the whiskey and ammunition."

"Could be," shrugged Rich. "I'm filing charges against the pack of 'em. Champion is a good talker; maybe he can get himself out of it."

"It's gonna take some tall talking," I said.

The next morning Rich rode on to Fort Sill and I returned to Cimarron. It was agreed that Pecos would bring in Clay Price later and hide him at Lula Belle's until the hearing.

We rode part of the way together, Rich and I, and he seemed in a high humor.

"It looks like we got it made, pardner," he gloated. "Seems to me Sheridan can't do less than give us protection the rest of the winter. We got enough stock; all we got to do is to watch 'em get fat and then count the pounds."

I nodded. Things did look rosy for the Cimarron Cattle Company.

"I've been figgering," he went on. "I owe close to forty thousand. I oughta come out with that much if the breaks are with me."

Forty thousand profit on a single winter's feeding!

"Then mebbe," he said slowly, "I can get in solid with Pat again. Mebbe when I own a place instead of leasing grass...."

I didn't want to discourage him. But I was sure in my own mind that Patricia would never consider him as a prospective husband. However, I thought, with Champion exposed, probably facing a prison sentence, she might change her notion.

I found Champion and Pat sitting together in the lobby talking in low voices. They used to play seven-up to pass away the time but of late they had just sat and talked. I nodded and hoped my face didn't show what I was thinking. It won't be long, I mused, until Mister Champion would need every one of those eloquent words of his. And I doubted if General Sheridan could be moved by oratory.

I started on upstairs but Martin called me back.

"Pete," he said, his face lit up by a smile, "I've been begging Patricia to let me tell you for a week."

"Tell me what?" I demanded with a faint heart. For I could tell by their expressions what he had to say.

"Patricia," he stated, "has done me the honor of consenting to be my wife."

I looked from one to the other. It wouldn't do, I thought, to spill the beans this early. Purdy and Mulloy might get Clay Price away from us. Martin Champion might be able to pull some trick out of his sleeve.

"When is the wedding?" I demanded.

"Oh, not for a month anyhow, Pete," Patricia said. "I want to go to Kansas City and buy a trousseau."

"And I have a house to build," Champion added happily. "It'll be the first house in Cimarron with glass windows."

I didn't say anything. I stood there and stared at the tips of my boots. So it wouldn't be for a month! Well, in less than a month Mister Champion's goose would be cooked in this Cimarron country. In a month's time Mister

Champion might be behind bars. Giving guns and whiskey to the Indians was plenty serious business.

I raised my eyes to his. There was a kind of pleading look on his face.

"I'll wait with my congratulations," I said crisply, "until the day of the wedding."

"Petey!" Patricia exclaimed in a distressed tone.

"Is that a threat, Pete, or a promise?" Champion asked in a low tone.

I grinned at him, and not pleasantly.

"Let's call it a hunch," I shrugged.

I started on upstairs; it was Pat who called me back this time.

"When will Rich be in, Pete? I want him to be the second to know."

"I couldn't say," I answered. "I think he rode over to Fort Sill."

"If it's to see Sheridan," Champion put in, "he wasted his ride. I'm expecting the General here any day."

I stared at him.

"Your side has lost, Pete," Champion said gently. "It was inevitable that you would."

"That's what you think," I snapped. "The shooting ain't over yet, Champion."

I heard Pat sob behind me as I stomped up the stairs. And I heard Martin try to comfort her:

"Don't worry, sweetheart," he said. "He's young. He'll get over it."

Yes, I thought. And damned sooner than you will!

# CHAPTER THIRTEEN

Rich rode in the next afternoon. He corroborated the story, that the General and his staff were on their way to Cimarron.

"Has Pecos brought in Price yet?" he asked.

I didn't know. I hadn't been to Lula Belle's that day. We walked down to the saloon and Pecos greeted us brightly.

"Yep," he nodded. "The galoot is back there in one of Lula Belle's rooms chained 'til he can hardly stir."

"Good," Rich said.

We had a drink with Lula Belle and she had to hear every detail of what we had to show Sheridan. Rich took the confession out of his wallet and I read it to her. I started to return it to him but he shook his head.

"You'll have to read it to the General," he shrugged. "You may as well keep it."

He leaned back in his chair and grinned at her. "You know, honey," he murmured, "you and me ain't got drunk together in a long time."

Her eyes lit up. "I'll open a bottle of champagne," she offered.

"You drink that," Rich chuckled. "Me for hard likker."

He squeezed my shoulder. "Get a good night's

sleep, pardner," he advised. "The General will get here tonight. We'll jump him out first thing in the morning."

I recalled Champion's words: "Your side has lost, Pete." I told them to Rich, but without explaining the circumstances under which the remark had been made. It was up to Pat to tell Rich, not me.

"I guess," I said, "Champion thinks he has something up his sleeve."

"He'd better have plenty," Rich said grimly.

I started toward the hotel. "Tell Luke I'll be down to eat about eight o'clock." Rich called after me. "Tell him I want chicken fried steak and fried potatoes, and they had better be just as I like 'em."

"I'll tell him," I agreed.

And, I grinned to myself, Rich would get 'em, too. Luke always fell over himself serving just what Rich wanted.

I was going into the hotel when I sighted the party of horsemen coming into town at a trot. I would have known 'em for soldiers even without their blue uniforms; no cowhands ever sat horses like that. They came on to the hotel and General Philip Sheridan dismounted.

I went on in ahead of him. Champion and Patricia were sitting side by side on the couch.

"I see the General is here," Martin said calmly.

I nodded. You danged fool, I thought, you

wouldn't be so pleased about it if you knew what I had in my pocket to show the General!

Sheridan stomped into the hotel. He had four officers with him, one captain and three lieutenants.

"Can you accommodate us?" he demanded of Luke.

Luke ran up to put the finishing touches on a room. While he waited Sheridan stood flicking his crop against his boots and staring around him, at Patricia and at Champion, and then at me. Champion came forward to shake hands. I turned and started up to my room. You won't get anywhere trying to butter him up, I thought. We'll lay the goods in front of him in the morning.

The General's voice stopped me.

"Young man!" he called.

"Yes, sir?"

He beckoned to me. I came slowly back down the stairs.

Sheridan turned to Luke. "Send warm water, sugar and whiskey to my room at once," he ordered. Luke hurried off and the General turned back to me: "Will you join me in a toddy, sir?"

His voice was crisp; Sheridan could not be genial even when issuing an invitation.

"Why, yes, sir," I mumbled, both shocked and flattered.

Then I wished I hadn't agreed so quickly. Evidently he had something to say to me, or to jump me about, for surely a general like Sheridan didn't just want the pleasure of my company.

He motioned to the stairs and followed me up, still flicking his crop against his boots. Inside his room, he loosened his tunic, unhooked his saber and dropped into the room's only chair, motioning me to sit on the bed.

"Is Mr. Stewart in town?"

"Why, yes, sir. He's down at the saloon."

Luke brought in the whiskey, water and sugar; General Sheridan mixed the toddys himself.

"Very good after a long ride," he explained. "To you, sir." He lifted his glass formally, then drained it at a gulp. He mixed another, but only sipped this one.

"Could I see Mr. Stewart tonight?" he asked.

"I could get him here in a minute," I said. I fingered the confession of Clay Price, which was in my shirt pocket. "We had hoped for a hearing in the morning, General."

"So I understand. But no need of it now. If I could see Mr. Stewart tonight, I could leave early in the morning. I am behind schedule as it is."

I frowned. This business couldn't be disposed of within a few minutes.

"I'll go get Rich," I said.

"Thank you, sir."

Rich came quickly when I told him General Sheridan insisted on talking to him that night.

"He has a notion," I explained, "that it will

only take a minute. But when we show him that paper . . ."

Rich nodded.

I was glad to observe that he did not show any effects of the liquor he had drunk. His step was firm and light when we entered the hotel. Pat and Champion were still on the sofa. Pat called to us as we started up the steps.

"Rich, can I see you a moment?"

He turned. I don't believe he had seen them there at all until she called to him.

"The General is waiting for us upstairs," I put in.

"We'll wait down here," Pat said. "I want to talk to you."

His eyes went from her to Martin Champion. "I'm sure I won't be long," he said slowly.

Maybe he guessed what she had to say to him, maybe he didn't.

Sheridan greeted him with the same crisp politeness. "Mr. Stewart, sir? A toddy?"

"Straight if you please, General," Rich answered.

Sheridan motioned for him to pour his own. The officer was smoking a black strong-smelling cigar and occasionally sipping his toddy. I sat back on the bed, Rich stood.

"General," Rich said, "I want to ask another hearing on my lease with the Arapahos. I have some evidence that . . ."

"No point of a hearing, Mr. Stewart," Sheridan interrupted. "I regret that I must inform you that your lease is cancelled as of today."

My shocked glance went from the General to Rich Stewart, then back again.

"What do you mean?" asked Rich. There was a snap in his voice. His weight rocked back and forth on his toes. "Since when are men convicted before they are heard?"

"Washington," he said in that same jerky way. "By orders of the new president."

"Cleveland!" I gasped.

"What's the story, sir?" Rich demanded.

"Grover Cleveland," Sheridan nodded. I could tell by his manner that he was no admirer of the new president. "All leases by individuals with Indians for grazing privileges are ordered cancelled," he went on, his voice now a low drone, "and the individuals are given sixty days to remove their possessions from the Indian territories."

"And there is no appeal!" Rich asked quietly.

"None," the General said firmly. "There is no point of your hearing now, sir. Whether or not the Cimarron Cattle Company is at fault in its relations with the Arapahos is of no consequence. The President's proclamation does not permit a loophole."

"Lemme get this straight?" Rich asked. "Not only is my lease cancelled, but I'm to get my cattle off the reservation within sixty days?"

"Such is the proclamation," Sheridan shrugged.

"What in the hell can I do with that many cattle in sixty days?" Rich snapped. "Can I find new grass for 'em in that time? Can I even get 'em to market? And what will the market be when I do? There is enough beef on Indian grass to send the price of cattle down to rock bottom."

The General nodded. "I realize that, sir," he murmured. "The price is already down."

"Doesn't this President—Cleveland, is it?—know what he is doing?"

"He did not confide in me, sir," Sheridan said crisply.

I fingered the confession of Clay Price.

"General," I appealed desperately, "something can be worked out surely. We have a witness who . . ."

"Hold it, Pete," Rich broke in, motioning for me to put Price's statement back in my pocket.

"General," he asked quietly, "there is no way out for me? No re-deal?"

"I'd say none, Mr. Stewart," was the firm answer. I think there was regret in Sheridan's tone.

The General studied the top of his glass. "I am a soldier, sir," he murmured. "I obey orders. The President made a mistake. He acted hurriedly upon the advice of men who assisted in his election. This order has created quite a stir. But he clearly has the constitutional authority to make such a proclamation stick. My advice to you, sir, is to rescue what you can."

"That will be danged little," Rich growled. "This ain't time to ship. If it could wait 'til spring . . ."

"A deputation of cattlemen waited upon the President, I understand," shrugged Sheridan. "He refused to extend the deadline. Sixty days from today, Mr. Stewart."

"Yes, sir," Rich said softly.

He turned to me. "We won't take up any more of the General's time, Pete," he murmured.

"Good night, Mr. Stewart," said Sheridan, standing. His small beady eyes gleamed. "I might add, sir—I *will* add it—that I would have shown you every personal consideration I could. I have spent most of my life on the frontier, sir. I know the type of men it takes to open up a country. I have dealt with other men like you, Mr. Stewart. With most of them I had very pleasant relations, considering, that is, I sometimes had a duty to perform that interfered with their ambitions. My congratulations to you, sir. You kicked open the door to the Cimarron."

"And now," Rich grinned ruefully, "I get kicked out of it."

He tilted his head in that funny way of his. "Thank you, General," he said.

Neither offered to shake hands. Rich turned to me again.

"Come along, Pete."

Outside, in the hallway, I caught Rich's shoulder. "Aren't you going to show the General the proof we got on Purdy and Mulloy?" I demanded.

"Why should I?" he shrugged.

He kept walking. "Downstairs," he said, "Patricia is waiting to tell me she wants to marry this Martin Champion."

"You know that!"

"I catch on to things," he murmured, "after so long."

They were waiting. Champion stood up but Rich waved him back to his seat.

"Yes?" he asked crisply.

"Rich," Patricia said slowly, "I am going to marry Martin."

The expression on his face did not change.

"I've wanted to tell you before," she said, her words falling in a rush from her lips, "but it was so hard. For so long we sorta took things so for granted. Then Martin came along . . . and I saw what I wanted, Rich. You like the open country. I like towns and a home and the security of an everyday life. There isn't much security with you, you know."

"No," he admitted, "there ain't."

He looked at Champion and his eyes hardened. "The General just told me I was kicked out. I guess I owe a lot of that to you?"

"I guess, Rich," Champion said slowly, "you owe it nearly all to me. Others helped, but I think the original proposal was mine. President Cleveland and my father were close friends. He promised me before the election that, if he won, he would cancel all leases with the Indians."

When Stewart did not answer for a moment, Martin went on: "There was nothing personal, Rich, believe that. Believe something else. When I heard the text of the President's proclamation, I telegraphed him myself protesting such an early deadline. I want you out of the Cimarron, Rich. But I never had any intentions of persecuting you."

"Sometimes," Rich murmured, "it's hard to tell about a man's motives."

He turned back to Pat.

"Rich," she begged, "don't look at me like that. Don't you see . . . I love you, but in a different way? How is it you always say it . . . you gotta play the cards like they fall. They fell this way, Rich. I'm sorry."

His face softened. "Dang your hide," he said with a smile touching his lean face, "you always do make a sucker out of me when you look like that."

He put on his hat, pulling the floppy brim down over his forehead. He grinned at her cheerfully.

"The best to you, Patricia," he told her.

"Rich, you darling!" she cried. She wanted to hug him but he pushed her off.

"No more of that," he said gruffly.

He whirled around and went clomping off. He slapped his hand against his thigh as he walked.

I looked after him, then to Champion.

"Some day," I told him coldly, "you'll hear from me how Rich is a better man than you are."

"Pete!" snapped Pat.

"And I'll tell you, too," I growled. "But not now. I got a compadre to see after."

And I hurried after Rich.

I overtook him just outside the saloon.

"Kinda late, ain't it, pardner?" he drawled. "Figured you'd want to stay at the hotel."

"I wanna get drunk with you," I said fiercely.

He laughed softly and put his arm around me. "Don't you worry about old Rich, pardner. I've been in tight spots before."

We took a table. Lula Belle finished a drink with one of the new store men, then came over. She was dressed in velvet again, with more than a hint of her full bosom revealed as she sat down and looked from Rich to me, and back again. The scar left by Poggin's gun butt still gleamed red; no layer of powder could hide it. But, I thought, she wasn't so bad off at that. Her scars were outside, where they showed. Rich Stewart's hurts were deep, down to the soles of his boots.

"Whose funeral is it?" Lula Belle demanded.

"Mine," Rich answered grimly. Then, his eyes softening and a grin breaking across his face: "And yours."

She listened quietly while he explained to her about the President's proclamation.

"Sixty days!" she mused. "We'll take quite a licking, Rich."

He nodded. "No telling what cattle will go down to," he observed gloomily. "If I could locate a range, and tide 'em over 'til spring . . ."

"You can try," Lula Belle snapped. "And another thing we can do; we can settle with Tim Mulloy, Bob Purdy and that Champion."

"No," Rich said slowly, "we can't do that."

I had waited anxiously for him to say definitely what would be done with Clay Price's confession.

"The hell we can't!" blazed Lula Belle. "That ain't like you, Rich."

"Champion," Rich told her, "is going to marry Patricia."

It took Lula Belle a moment to understand. "She's ditching you!" she exclaimed.

Rich nodded.

"And you're sucker enough to cover him up!" she stormed, her bosom heaving. "Rich Stewart, that is the biggest fool thing I ever heard of."

"I reckon," he admitted, his lips tightening. "I reckon I'm the biggest fool you ever knew, Lula Belle."

"Look, Rich Stewart," she snapped. "I've got

something to say about this. It was Champion's idea to hire that Al Poggin to come here and clean up the town. Champion paid Poggin's expenses out of his pocket. And you can see what Poggin did to me? Do you think I wanna be easy on Martin Champion after that?"

"I reckon," Rich admitted, "it comes hard."

He stirred and poured himself a drink. "Her dad was my amigo, honey," he pointed out. "Frank Haines set me on the right trail. Frank gave me a horse and a goldpiece and told me he was backing my play. She's Frank Haines' gal, Lula Belle. I couldn't throw the loop that would get him in a jam even if I wanted to."

"What about Mulloy? What about Purdy?"

"I couldn't bring charges against one without involving 'em all," Rich shrugged. "I'll tell the boys to let Clay go. He can fan the breeze for all I care. This paper Pete wrote up—we'll tear it up."

"Like hell!" stormed Lula Belle. "What about my thirty thousand dollars, Rich Stewart? Can you just tear that up, too?"

"It's a debt," he admitted quietly. "I'll pay it off when I can."

Her eyes were suddenly bright with a stony glint. She felt of the scar on her forehead.

"If you won't file charges," she said, "I will. This time, Rich Stewart, you don't get your own way."

He shook his head. "I'll start looking around for grass in the morning," he said tonelessly. "I'll start the boys rounding up. We'll get out what we can. All that's there is yours, Lula Belle."

He hesitated a moment, then added in a voice that left no doubt as to his determination:

"And that, Lula Belle, is all there is."

"I won't be a sucker again, Rich," she said in a lower voice. Her tone was calm but her bosom still heaved and the rush of blood to her forehead made the scar burn a rich purple in color. "You've had me jumping through a hoop since the day you walked into my place in Ellsworth. All I've made out of other men—made the hard way—I've given you."

He started to protest; she stopped him with a wave of her hand. "I know," she said wearily. "You made it clear from the start how you stood. I ain't whining, Rich. I'm just looking after little Lula Belle like I should have been doing all along. You owe me thirty thousand dollars, Rich, out of the Cimarron Cattle Company. There are some odds and ends but I'll settle for that. If you don't want me to go to General Sheridan with Clay Price's confession, you'd better pay it within sixty days."

"You don't have Clay's confession," Rich pointed out.

She nodded. "But you're turning it over to me right now," she said crisply. "That's the advance deposit. Else I see General Sheridan in the morning."

Rich looked at her with eyes that seemed to have sunk way back in his head. "You'll never squeal to Sheridan," he muttered. "I'd kill you first. You know that."

She held out her hand. "Gimme the confession," she demanded.

"No," Rich snapped.

But Rich had overlooked one thing. *I* had the confession, not he. I handed it across the table to Lula Belle. Rich grabbed for it but Lula Belle snatched it and thrust it into her full bosom.

"There it is," I told her. "You're going to be treated fair. Maybe Rich owes us something but you don't. If the cattle don't bring enough, we'll dig up the rest. It'll be up to Champion to help."

Lula Belle's expression changed when she looked at me. "I ain't trying to be unreasonable, Pete," she choked. "I've loved this long-legged fool, Pete. I loved him so much that I'd give my money and anything else I have to see him happy. But I'm not in a notion to play gentle with this Martin Champion. And your sister . . . when she turned him down, she threw away her claim on him."

She turned back to Rich and the scar on her forehead blazed again.

"I guess that's news to you," she snapped, "that I was in love with you. I reckon you thought I was backing you because I saw a chance to make a dollar."

He took a long while answering. First he rolled a cigarette. Then, through the partial cover of its smoke, he murmured:

"No, Lula Belle, I knew it. I've known it a long time."

# CHAPTER FOURTEEN

Rich was gone for two weeks, riding through the north Texas country looking for new range. But others were before him—the Reid brothers from the Mescalero country, the Hill and Manning combine from Wyoming. He came back with the gloomy order to work the cows north. There we would bring them together into one herd and drive them on to Kansas.

The market had slumped some but the bottom had not fallen out of it; Rich would clear out with his hide. He borrowed another four thousand from Patricia and me and he had eighty riders combing the hills. He made me straw boss of one crew and the men were tickled over it rather than resentful. They called me the "kid ramrod." But kid or kidder, we worked hard. Sixty days wasn't much time. It was from sunup until after sundown for us.

Pecos Sherrill's outfit joined mine on the fifty-eighth day and we could be proud of the stock we had rounded up. We had fully five thousand head. If the others had done as well, Rich would come with a stake.

"Where did all your cattle come from?" I demanded of Pecos.

He grinned, "Ain't they all wearing our brand?"

I observed the calves which didn't have a mother. "Pecos, you musta latched onto every calf in that end of the reservation?"

"My conscience ain't hurting me none," he shrugged. "Mebbe we did pick up a few of Purdy's calves by mistake, I wouldn't know."

There were five outfits and now, the day before the deadline, we were converging upon the valley Rich had picked for our final roundup. Pecos and I were the first two straw bosses there. And a Captain Blair Hudson rode up with several troopers.

"General Sheridan has instructed me to show you every courtesy," he explained. Then, unbending with a smile: "That means he isn't taking official notice if you're a few days late. You're doing everything in your power to get out in sixty days and that is all he asks."

"I think we'll make it," I said.

For the other outfits weren't far away. The next afternoon their lead cows came sniffing into the valley where we were hastily slapping brands on the unmarked stock.

"What's this for?" Rich demanded suspiciously as he rode up and observed our branding crew at work.

"Branding cows," drawled Pecos. "Never heard of it, did you?"

Rich took in the situation at a glance. Some of this was young stock and never had been branded. But some of the calves were mighty old to be called such.

Rich started to climb down off his horse. Pecos jabbed an indignant finger in his direction.

"Dang you, Rich," growled Pecos, "don't go around sticking your nose into my business. I brought them cows out of your country and you got my word for it they're your stock."

"Your word?" grinned Rich.

"Don't call me a liar," snapped Pecos.

Rich hesitated, then shrugged his shoulders. "*Bueno*," he said. "But I never heard of cows dropping so many calves."

We had the herd milling around on the sixtieth day. Rich estimated there were twelve thousand head. The latest figure from Kansas City was about four bucks a head, the way our cattle would weigh out, and unless the market took a bad turn before we got into Kansas, Rich was clear with a few thousand to boot.

Rich grinned at me. "Am I right, pardner," he demanded, "or am I loco? Ain't we got enough cows here to pay off Lula Belle and start another outfit?"

"We got some cows," I agreed. I winked at Pecos. "Some visitors maybe," I added dryly. "Some of the cows down by the river just raised hell to come along with us. Seemed to be right attached to our yearlings and I couldn't bear to separate 'em."

"I believe that danged kid," grinned Pecos, "stole more of Purdy's stock than I did."

"I'm just a kid," I pointed out. "I don't know one brand from another."

Captain Hudson and his troopers rode off that night. Again the officer assured us that Sheridan would be cooperative.

"We'll wait for a change of weather then," Rich said, "before starting our drive."

Hudson assured him that the General would have no objections to that.

Rich paid off our extra hands and we settled down to wait for the weather to clear. The sky was getting ready for something; it looked like so many granite sheets stacked dizzily on top of each other. The air was still, like the pools in a slow-running river. We drove the cows about eight miles north and settled down in the main bunkhouse to wait out nature.

The next morning a crew of men rode down upon us. There were four of them. Their straw boss was an albino, a ruddy-faced man whose contrasting coloring made him look like a side-show freak. He said he was Bill Tipton and he was working for an outfit starting up in Wyoming.

"We can use some cows," he explained. "The boss sent me down here to make a deal with you."

"I'm ready to deal," nodded Rich. "You boys light and come on in."

It was crowded in the dugout with the Wyoming men.

"Who's you with?" Rich asked, pouring a drink.

"New man," was the evasive answer. "I'll take four thousand head, Stewart."

"What price?"

"The market is about four. It should go down a buck in about thirty days. I'll pay you ten if I can cull 'em."

My heart leaped. So, I knew, did Rich Stewart's despite his poker face.

"Some of this," Rich murmured, "is prime stuff. They're fat. They can take the winter."

The albino chuckled and handed his tin cup to Pecos to be refilled from the whiskey jug.

"Stewart," he grinned, "you know you're gonna take ten a head and never look back. Why the palaver?"

"It ain't clear in my own mind," shrugged Rich. "Where are you trailing? Is it cash?"

Tipton reflected a moment. "Know where Sedalia is?"

"Sure," Rich nodded.

"It would be on our way," the albino explained, "to turn off there. I'll mosey on ahead and pick a full crew. We'll take 'em at Dugan's store."

"Cash there?" demanded Rich.

"Yes."

Rich studied Tipton with a suggestion of a

smile on his lean face. "Not many albinos in this country," he murmured. "Talk spreads about 'em."

"Yeah?" snapped Tipton, his face losing its ruddy good humor.

I wondered at Rich. It wasn't the way of a cow camp to speculate upon rumors about a man's past.

"An albino," went on Stewart, "could no more dodge that talk that he can fly to the moon. I wouldn't have known your name, Tipton, though I reckon I've heard it before. But I don't reckon there could be two of 'em operating in this country."

I stared from one expressionless face to the other. There was no way to tell whether Rich was riled up or not. He'd talk that softly and that slowly if haranguing with another Al Poggin.

The albino rolled a smoke before answering. "I never heard of another one," he said finally. "As you say, Stewart, talk flies about albinos."

A grin broke the stiffness of his face. "Every time I hit an Indian camp the squaws are waiting for me," he admitted.

"Reckon so," Rich nodded. He poured a drink. Then suddenly there was a snap in his voice:

"Whose orders are you taking now—Purdy's or Mulloy's?" he demanded.

"Mulloy's," the albino answered calmly. "Purdy and me, we split up. Mulloy is a different kind of hombre." Then, as if for my benefit: "Some may not like the way he forks a bronk but he gets 'em gentled."

Rich brooded a minute. Now I could understand his indecision. It hadn't occurred to me that this offer of ten bucks per head had come from Tim Mulloy. Me, I wouldn't have touched the offer with a ten-foot pole. But, after a long wait, Stewart bobbed his head.

"Ten a head is *bueno*, if in cash," he said curtly. "We'll cut 'em out for you at Sedalia. If you or your tally man is there, you can make the cut yourself. If you ain't I'll do the best I can for you."

"If I ain't there," agreed the albino, "you make the cut. Your money will be waiting for you at Dugan's Store. Cash."

The next morning Tipton rode off with his men. I could hardly wait to get Rich off to himself.

"That forty thousand," I said excitedly, "will put you over the hump. From Dugan's on, pardner, it's a downhill pull."

He shook his head. "We ain't out of the woods yet," he said gloomily. "There will be snow by night."

There was. Gentle snow at first, just trickling. Then faster and bigger and faster.

We worked past dark pulling up mesquite roots, stripping every kind of a tree and gathering cow chips. A blue snorter was coming and no fooling.

A brush corral behind the sod camp would keep the horses out of the full force of the gale and we worked some of the cattle down from the slopes into the creek flats.

It was ten o'clock when we called it a night. The sheet-iron stove was roaring out with everything it had but still it was chilly inside the camp. Cherry was cook for the night and the steaks he cut helped warm our innards. But a man's back and front were never warm at once.

We sat up 'til midnight. We piled on everything we had for cover but still a bunk was no protection. We lay awake and talked of how cold it must be getting. It had been even a little warm that afternoon; here twelve hours later it must be hitting close to zero.

I must have dozed off, for nearly everybody was up when next I heard a hum of voices.

"They'll be all right 'til time for the sun to come up." I heard Black John protesting. "Cows can take one night. It's when they start moving that they go out like Lottie's eye. They work up a little sweat foraging and that body moisture freezes and, if they lie down again, they ain't got long to live. In a couple of hours maybe we got work to do."

I rolled out of the bunk and pulled on my boots. I hadn't taken off anything else.

Rich sat quiet and brooding over a cup of coffee. I poured some for myself, and the scalding liquid felt good in the cold of my throat and chest.

"If they can keep moving," Black John went on in the same know-it-all fashion, "they can live for days. I've seen 'em drift with the storm for that long without food or water and live through it."

I looked at my watch. It was only five o'clock.

Black John now looked straight at Rich. "That drift fence needs to be cut in at least two places," he murmured. "Cut it at both ends and it will go down with the first big push."

Rich had nothing to say. It wasn't like him to sit stone-quiet and disinterested. His eyes turned in my direction but they didn't see me.

I wanted to get close to him, to sit next to him. It was pretty plain what he was thinking. He didn't believe those cattle of his had a snowball's chance in hell. There was a droop to the corners of his mouth that I had never seen before. I ducked my head. This danged blizzard was wiping him out. And he had more to worry about than just money. There was Lula Belle and her threat of filing charges against Bob Purdy, Tim Mulloy, Jenson and Martin Champion.

I couldn't blame him for slumping in his chair like a whipped dog. Twelve hours before it had looked like he could rake in a few white chips out of loser's pot. I had heard about 'em— losers' pots. The winners tossed out a few whites magnanimously and those already wiped out played a showdown hand for the crumbs.

With the cattle we had rounded up, and that rather queer offer from the albino, he would have ended up with something. Then the blizzard hit. Two days and he would have been clear. But there weren't two days. And, as he looked at Black John, a glaze over his eyes, it was clear that he didn't believe that it would do any good to cut the drift fence.

"No kind of cattle," he said in a dull voice, "can stand this weather. They'd freeze walking. I've seen some weather myself. A cow is a dumb critter. Sucks in cold when it's hungry and thirsty. No use to cut the drift fence."

Nobody spoke for a moment. Black John looked around him. He had been the spokesman of these riders when they had served notice on Rich Stewart that they had to be paid a cash bonus or else. He was a lone wolf man and there was no use for Rich to think that Black John paid him a personal loyalty. John didn't. But he was a cowhand.

"You sabbe cattle, Stewart," Black John said in a grim tone. "You sabbe cattle plenty. You own 'em. You got us paid up. We got no kick coming."

He jumped to his feet and walked close to the stove and spread his hands to its warmth.

"But where I came from they never gave up a

herd," he snapped. "That fence has gotta be cut, Stewart."

He took a step toward Rich.

"We'll cut it," he proposed harshly. "You and me, we'll cut her down."

Rich studied him a moment. "Takes two to cut a fence," he murmured tonelessly. "One to cut, one to hold. Needs to be cut at both corners. It would take four of us, two to a corner."

John turned to the keg which three of the boys had been using as a poker table and took the greasy deck of cards. He shuffled them swiftly, then replaced them on the keg.

"Cut," he said tersely. "Two low men."

It was clear that he meant for all of us to be dealt in. Pecos reached out and turned up a four. Then I flicked over the deuce of clubs.

"Cut again," Black John said, taking the card from me. "This is no weather for a button."

"No," I refused firmly. "Rich and me will take the lower corner."

Rich looked up at me a moment in the same unseeing fashion. Then he pushed back his stool.

"Sure," he nodded, and that old-time gleam came back to his eyes. "Pete and me will cut the lower corner."

Pecos was second low with a four. We pulled on our slickers and mackinaws. Those staying behind pushed their wraps upon us. I thought I had on enough clothes to shut out any gale, but when I stepped outside I found the wind was blowing right through me.

Heads down, we stumbled among the horses hobbled in the brush corral. My fingers were numbed by the time we had tightened our saddle cinches.

"We'll cut the corner first," Rich yelled in my ear. "We'll need the fence to find our way in."

I rode close to him, huddled over the horse to dodge as much of the gale as I could. The wind was behind us as we could see ahead. Daylight had come but no sun pierced this sheet of driving snow and ice.

We rode among bunches of cows slogging south, their heads down, their moans sounding out above the roar of the wind. They were already more dead than alive, that was plain to be seen. Fence or no fence, this herd wouldn't pull through.

But I felt like Black John did. We had to cut the fence. We couldn't rest easy 'til we did that.

Rich was ahead of me. He motioned for me to ride to his lee. I tried to grin but my lips wouldn't move. He didn't have his tail between his legs now.

We would have known when we reached the fence corner even if we couldn't have seen clear enough with the gale behind us, for there were a hundred cattle at least bunched there against the coulee. They weren't stamping or pushing, just standing there huddled against each other. They would freeze that way, on their feet.

Rich tried to yell something at me but his words were whipped out of his mouth and blown far south before I could make 'em out. Then he gestured. I followed him out of the saddle and along the wire. We snipped the fence on one side, circled around the coulee, cut it again on the far side. We couldn't crowd in among the paralyzed cows to cut down the corners.

Rich lurched back to his horse. When I tried to follow him the blizzard's force almost swept me back. He came toward me pulling my mount and, with the horse as a temporary shelter, I climbed into the saddle.

I followed him into the bunched cattle. We swung quirts and fired our guns. Finally they lumbered into motion. The motion spread until we were being tossed back and forth by the rush of cows from behind us. A heavy mass hit me and almost knocked my horse down. It was Rich fighting his way to me.

He caught my bridle and held both of our horses together.

We had cut the fence. We had started the dying cattle moving. But now we were caught plumb in the middle of our own stampede!

Wildly I grabbed for Rich's saddlehorn as bawling cattle pressed behind me. My horse screamed and jumped, probably from a sharp horn. We couldn't turn back or to either side.

But if we kept close together, the weight of two horses and two men pressing back stoutly, maybe . . .

I clung to Rich's saddlehorn; he pulled tightly on my bridle. We rode out the wave that way, thrown back and forth, often held up only by the weight of the steers, but held up.

Then suddenly there was no force behind us but the gale and that we could turn into. Rich pulled ahead, still holding my bridle. He and his mount made a windbreak as they shuffled forward into the face of the blizzard.

How he found his way I'll never know. But by noon we were back in camp and eager hands, if rough ones, pulled away our clothes and bathed our faces, ears, hands and feet with water. They started off with snow, then ended up with water scalding hot. A few drinks of whiskey and we were finally breathing the warmth of the sheet-iron stove instead of the icy air outside.

Pecos and Black John had beaten us back. Black John was the first man to talk about what he had seen.

"Reckon it was a fool thing to do," he said after a long while, "going out like that. We got 'em to running but they'll never make it. There won't be enough of 'em alive by night to have a good roping."

That look came back to Rich's face again. But

it didn't stay there long. His lips parted in a grin.

"That's the trouble with this danged game," he said. "Every time a man gets caught bluffing, he loses."

We rode at a jog trot back to Cimarron. Around us were hundreds of brown smears where cattle had fallen, or had been trampled down, and hadn't gotten up. Rich wouldn't even zigzag through the open looking for any bunches that might be alive.

We got to town in mid-afternoon. I started to pull in at the hotel but Rich insisted I go on to Lula Belle's for a drink.

I followed him inside the saloon. He hadn't breathed a word of what he intended to do about the account Lula Belle insisted must be paid. He sauntered in calmly as if he didn't have a worry in the world. I couldn't follow his pattern. I dreaded looking Lula Belle in the eyes.

She was playing solitaire at a corner table. She raised her head, gave us only a swift glance, then returned her attention to the cards on the table before her. I saw Rich's mouth quirk at the corners.

I nodded to the bartender that I wanted the same thing as Rich. We took a swallow, then turned to face the other men in the saloon.

I saw him first. I nudged Rich.

The albino man, Bill Tipton, was drinking at a table with Tim Mulloy.

Now Tim slowly pushed back his chair and came toward us at a lazy walk. There was no expression on his leathery face. I had never seen any there except when his countenance was aflame with his hatred for a Haines.

It wasn't now. He nodded to me first. I did not return his greeting. Then stepped in between me and Rich.

He didn't say a word for a long moment. We did not offer him a drink, he did not ask us to drink with him. Rich stood watching him with half-closed eyes and hands low with elbows hooked, as if half-expecting trouble.

"It was hell, wasn't it?" Mulloy asked after a moment.

"Some," Rich shrugged.

"Wiped out, ain't you?"

"Yes."

Mulloy licked his lips. "Got word of that hombre named Price," he murmured.

"Did you?"

Tim turned on Rich. "Got any plans for that confession of his, Rich?"

"I don't even have it."

Mulloy looked down at the floor. "I had a hate, Stewart," he said slowly. "I reckon I overplayed my hand. I got no favors coming to me, least of all from you. But I wanna make one deal with you, Stewart."

"What?" Rich demanded brusquely.

"The button's sister there," Mulloy said, pointing to me, "is marrying Martin Champion. Champion was in with us some, Stewart. He was out to break your lease with the Arapahos. But he didn't know anything about the whiskey and the guns. He didn't know we were prodding up Icado. I kept that from him. He wouldn't have stood for it."

I looked hopefully to Rich. I had been thinking some on my own. It wasn't like Champion to be in on a deal like that. Many things might be wrong with him, but he didn't strike me as either a cheat or a liar. He was an honorable man, and proud of it.

"That's easy to swallow," Rich said carefully.

"Me and Purdy and Jenson," Mulloy went on, "we're guilty as hell. I guess I lost my head, Stewart. I never was a cheap crook before. But I had a hate on."

He licked his lips. "I ain't running from you, Stewart," he said. "I've given you the tally. Make your play, but leave Champion out of it."

I held my breath. I didn't want Rich to take up the fight Tim Mulloy offered him. Tim Mulloy had hounded my father to his grave and had been an enemy of my family's since the day of my birth. But it took guts to stand there and face Rich Stewart with that confession. Rich Stewart could drop him with a six-gun and Tim Mulloy knew it. There was a tingle of whiteness in Tim's lean face. He thought he was only a minute away from death, a death he admitted he deserved.

I was afraid he was, too. I had seen Rich look like that before. I had seen his eyes gleam and his lips quirk and lines of amusement break the leathery mask of his face . . . and a minute later, in the same calm way, blazing death would leap up from his hip.

"Your tally is *bueno*," he said finally. "Champion is out of it."

I turned to Lula Belle. She had dropped her deck of cards. She was staring at the two men who leaned against her bar.

"Purdy and Jenson," Rich shrugged, "they're rats. If the chance ever comes, I'll pistol-whip 'em. I wouldn't flatter 'em by calling 'em worth a fight."

It seemed to me Mulloy's face went paler still. But he waited calmly and his hand on the bar didn't quiver.

Rich turned away from Tim's intent eyes. He bent his head a moment. Then he spun a gold coin on the bar.

"My pardner and I were fixing to have a drink," he said calmly. "Care to wet your whistle, Tim?"

I gasped. This came too sudden for me. It left Tim Mulloy limp, too.

Rich didn't wait for his answer. "Three whiskeys," he told the barkeep.

Two pair of hands shook, no more. The quivering fingers belonged to myself and the bartender.

Rich bent his head again. He stared into the glass before him.

"Frank would have wanted it that way, Tim," he murmured, his voice so low that only Mulloy and I heard him. "The feud was buried with him. He was always willing to pay that price. Remember?"

"Yeah," nodded Mulloy, his voice harsh. He toyed with his glass. He turned to me.

"Mind, son?" he asked in a hoarse whisper. "To him . . . your dad."

We drank. The whiskey—or something—made all three of us cough.

Then Rich turned away with a careless "be seeing you, Tim." He turned and walked to Lula Belle's table.

I followed him slowly. I wasn't sure that I belonged there. Rich crushed the cigarette he was smoking under his heel. He pulled up a chair and sat across from her. I stood, staring at her, observing the exposed slopes of her bosom, wondering what would be her reaction to Rich Stewart's report that not a head of cattle had been salvaged, and that he had only a few goldpieces toward payment of the debt she held.

She didn't look up until she had finished her game, throwing in with only five cards out. Then she studied him with an unblinking gaze for a moment before she spoke.

"Well!"

There was defiance in her voice and bitterness. He held out his hand.

"Gimme Price's confession?" he demanded.

"No."

"Yes, Lula Belle," he insisted quietly.

For a moment her gaze fought his. Then she bent her head and, with a choking sound, took the paper out of her bosom.

"Damn you, Rich," she sobbed, now burying her face on the table.

He chuckled. "Lula Belle," he teased, "you're a sucker. You're the biggest sucker in the world. Me, I'm just a poor second."

"Don't, Rich, please," she begged.

"You'd do anything I say, wouldn't you?" he demanded.

"Of course, you damned long-legged . . . !"

"Then how long," he asked, "will it take you to clear out of here?"

She raised her tearful face.

"Why?"

"I've been here too long," he murmured. "Both of us have. I'm trying Wyoming. Taking off like a sage hen. How long before you can get ready?"

Her eyes showed plainly that she was daring to hope, but that she was holding herself back.

"What do you mean, Rich?" she asked quietly.

"Another deal like this, no. I'm through dealing with you."

"Like hell you are," he snapped, but with a grin. "You're marrying me and that's one deal you gotta see through."

"Rich," she demanded, pushing her chair back, "are you crazy?"

"I've been crazy," he admitted. "I think I'm kinda coming to my senses all of a sudden."

He gazed around at the gilt and garnish of her saloon.

"What do we do with this?" he asked. "Burn it or just ride off and leave it?"

She let his question lie a moment while she studied his face. Then, calmly, only a hint of a smile on her full red lips, she motioned to the barkeep.

"Drinks around, Tony," she called. "Everybody belly up. On the house."

She didn't have to invite 'em twice. They were always ready for that.

"And keep pouring 'em Tony," she added, "until it's gone."

She came to her feet. Her full breasts strained at their meager covering as she waved her arms.

"Everybody belly up," she repeated. "Send the word out on the street. We're leaving a good taste in the mouths of Cimarron, Rich Stewart and me."

Rich and I came to our feet, too. Lula Belle

called to the stolid-faced Indian who cleaned up and did odd jobs around the saloon.

"Saddle me a horse, Chincy," she ordered. "*Muy* pronto."

Then she turned back to Rich.

"We'll just ride off and leave it," she said with a catch in her voice. "Burning it would take more time than I figure on wasting."

I grabbed Rich in a bear hug.

"Pardner," I congratulated him, "that blizzard blew some sense into your noggin. Lemme grab a change of clothes and I'll be right with you."

I grabbed the bottle Tony brought us and poured a drink. "Here's to Wyoming!" I proposed.

Rich took the glass out of my hand before I could take a sip.

"No, pardner," he said gently. "You ain't going."

"Not going!" I gasped. "Rich!"

Lula Belle put her arm around me. "No, Petey," she said gently. "You belong here."

"Like hell," I snapped, throwing off the arm. "We're pardners, aren't we?"

Rich looked away from my appeal. "Your dad didn't want you riding one trail after another, Pete," he said. "He told me that when I headed this way. When you ride hills, Rich, he told me, you gotta ride light and you gotta ride alone. And when you get to the hilltop, Rich, you'll find that all you got is what you brought with you."

He caught my shoulder. "Remember how that speech took with the General?" he asked. "Remember what he said about me kicking open the door to the Cimarron? Well, pardner, lemme ride off thinking I kicked it open for you . . . and Pat . . . and Champion."

"*Bueno*," I choked. He wouldn't take me so I might as well pretend to take it in good spirits.

"Sure," I added. "Sure. So long, pardner."

He handed my drink back to me. "Don't you want to stick around and see us off?" he demanded. "Don't you wanna drink to us . . . and Wyoming?"

"No," I said firmly. "So long, Rich."

He nodded. He lifted his hand in a gesture I remembered from a long time ago. And I walked out of the saloon without a backward look.

But I did see them ride away. I was watching from the hotel window as they rode by. I was standing there, shaking a little, when somebody said in my ear:

"You'll miss him, Pete."

It was Martin Champion. I nodded.

"Yeah," I admitted, "I'll miss him."

His hand fell lightly on my shoulder. "I'll never make up for Rich Stewart," he said gently. "But help me try, will you?"

I nodded.

And he did try. When he started other newspapers as the Cimarron country grew, he made me a partner. And he sat with me through two awful nights when my first baby was born and it seemed for a while that girl I had married—the nester girl who had made a face at me from the seat of her wagon—might not pull through.

He never knew that Clay Price had signed a confession in Rich Stewart's camp that would have put the quietus on his political ambitions before they were ever born. That and all that went with it went riding off into Wyoming.

Nor did he ever know where the money came from that was poured into his race for governor. I did. Tim Mulloy never went back to Texas. As far as I know, he never met Patricia face to face again, and the only thing he had for me when we passed on the street was a nod.

But I knew that Tim Mulloy rode from line camp to line camp talking to cowmen in his harsh-voiced way, and the way that Martin Champion carried the cow country upset his opponent's apple cart.

He was a good governor. I was proud of him and I learned, by slow stages, to admire him. He stood by me through every crisis that ever came up. And, settling down like I did, a newspaper publisher and a family man instead of a hard and fast galoot, I was through riding rivers anyhow.

**Center Point Large Print**
600 Brooks Road / PO Box 1
Thorndike, ME 04986-0001 USA

(207) 568-3717

US & Canada:
1 800 929-9108
www.centerpointlargeprint.com